"YOU WANT ME TO RETIRE?"

"Yes! You can't be a jockey forever, Tracy. As it is you have to starve yourself to maintain your proper riding weight, and it's ruining your health."

"I won't give it up!" Tracy yelled. "I've worked for years to ride at the big tracks and get decent mounts. You can't expect me to throw it all over for nothing!"

"Not for nothing. For *me*. When will you get it through your thick head that I love you? I don't care if you're a top jockey or not. All I want is for us to be together."

"Just listen to me, Mark Flanagan," she said coldly and quietly. "I'm finally doing just what I've always wanted to do, and nobody—not even you—is going to take it away from me."

CANDLELIGHT ECSTASY ROMANCES®

RACE THE
WIND

Veronica Flynn

A CANDLELIGHT ECSTASY ROMANCE®

Published by
Dell Publishing Co., Inc.
1 Dag Hammarskjold Plaza
New York, New York 10017

Dell ® TM 681510, Dell Publishing Co., Inc.

Candlelight Ecstasy Romance®, 1,203,540, is a registered
trademark of Dell Publishing Co., Inc., New York, New York.

ISBN: 0-440-17232-2

Printed in the United States of America

April 1986

10 9 8 7 6 5 4 3 2 1

WFH

To Our Readers:

We have been delighted with your enthusiastic response to Candlelight Ecstasy Romances®, and we thank you for the interest you have shown in this exciting series.

In the upcoming months we will continue to present the distinctive sensuous love stories you have come to expect only from Ecstasy. We look forward to bringing you many more books from your favorite authors and also the very finest work from new authors of contemporary romantic fiction.

As always, we are striving to present the unique, absorbing love stories that you enjoy most—books that are more than ordinary romance. Your suggestions and comments are always welcome. Please write to us at the address below.

Sincerely,

The Editors
Candlelight Romances
1 Dag Hammarskjold Plaza
New York, New York 10017

CHAPTER ONE

"That's it, kid, that's it—keep 'er goin'—you're doin' great! That's it—hug the rail—she loves the rail. You're almost there—one more furlong. Come on—yeah! You've done it!"

Scotty MacDougall hit his stopwatch: one minute and eight seconds for six furlongs. "Fantastic— what a horse; what a jockey!" He pushed his cap back and wiped his brow with the cuff of his jacket and exposed the beginnings of a balding, freckled scalp, with unkempt fiery red hair shooting out above his ears and down the nape of his neck. Scotty MacDougall was messy, but one of the best trainers in the business. He hit the rail enthusiastically, several times, with his tweed cap and yelled, "You're a winner, kid!"

Tracy pulled up alongside of him, panting, and patted the horse's withers, all the while leaning over and whispering encouraging words into Becket's ear.

"You are a prize; I knew you'd do it for me," Tracy said. The horse whinnied as if in response to her words.

"I knew you could do it, kid," Scotty yelled as Tracy jumped off the horse. "I always said that horse had potential; even your ol' man agreed, but you, kid, you're the one who pushed her all the

9

way. One minute and eight, geez, right on the nose! I'm so bloody proud of ya," he cried and whacked Tracy across the rump.

Tracy whirled sharply and stared at him in annoyance.

"Don't do *that;* I don't like it, Scotty," she said firmly, pulling off the sweaty riding cap, releasing long red hair that cascaded to her shoulders. Her green eyes were flashing furiously, and she turned and headed for the stables. As she charged through the damp, early morning mist, the cold air made her breath visible.

Rushing after her, with Becket in tow, Scotty finally reached her, and took her by the shoulders. He looked up at her. Scotty was five feet two inches; Tracy was five feet five inches—tall by jockey's standards, but slim as a reed. She fought to stay that way.

"Aw, don't get so uppity, lass; it's just a friendly, good luck pat. I treat all the boys . . ."

She turned and faced him squarely. "Well, in case you've forgotten I'm *not* one of the boys. She broke away and continued walking.

"Hey, come on, 'Trace,' I've known you too long —forever!—since you were a kid . . ."

"That's just it." She turned. "I'm not a kid anymore."

The pink horizon was slowly pushing the steel, somber gray of the cold night behind the trees that bordered the Belmont Race Track. She faced forward, held her head imperiously, and walked off, her expensive leather boots kicking at random at the pebbles that mingled with the twigs and green patches of grass. She hated the condescension that many of the men around the track showed her, and she shouldn't snap at him. She knew Scotty didn't mean anything—still . . .

Scotty raced after her, but Becket snorted her disapproval at being pulled along—she had done enough racing for one morning. Scotty was panting; he wasn't as slim as he had been when he rode five years ago. He had developed a little pot, and Tracy had playfully labeled him the "Little Buddha." He didn't mind—he was crazy about her—the best woman rider he'd ever seen. He could never really be angry with her—anybody who could ride the way she could—he could forgive her anything. Besides, he knew why she was tense.

"Hey, Tracy, wait up, will ya? The Little Buddha is having a tough time pulling this load. Have a heart, lass." He could hear a little snicker when he referred to himself as the Buddha.

Scotty MacDougall had been born in Scotland and came to the States when he was fifteen. He started riding a year later, and Tracy's father was the first one to give him a break. He never forgot it; and when he just couldn't keep his weight down anymore—and was losing more mounts—he knew it was time to toss in his cap. Cornelius "Bull" Morgan wouldn't let him feel sorry for himself, and told him to get his tail movin' and start training, that he needed another good trainer. Scotty turned his energies to training for Morgan's stable.

He loved horses, and the alliance had been a firm one for years. He loved old Morgan, and he loved Morgan's daughter—the feisty Irish beauty, too, but—well, that could never be. That was Scotty's little secret. At least he could be near her and help her become the best woman "jock" this country had ever seen. But, she was cut right from the old man's boots: she had a temper to match her beauty; brains, too. But best of all, she had a natural talent for riding. She could handle a horse just like a man!

He puffed up the slight incline toward the stables. "C'mon, 'Trace,' wait for the Buddha . . ."

He could hear her laughter and she turned to face him, kicking at the cones that had fallen from the pine trees.

"What's eatin' you anyway, kid? You know you can talk to me, lass."

"Oh, Scotty," she said with a smile. "I'm sorry. It's not you—it's me." She shoved her hands in her pockets and looked up. "And stop calling me kid. I'm twenty-five; all the other apprentices are seventeen and eighteen. I feel like an old lady. Maybe I should carry a cane instead of a whip."

Scotty laughed but said nothing; he knew she had to talk, and it was seldom that Tracy Morgan invited anyone into her private world.

"It's just that I'm so nervous about my first race —just two days away . . ."

Scotty put his free hand out to her and flicked some dirt from her jacket. "Don't be silly, kid." He paused and added, "Sorry, lass, to me you'll always be a kid." He rubbed his protuberant belly affectionately and looked at her staring at her feet. "What of it?" he asked. He released Becket's reins and let her walk into her stall. He closed the half-gate behind him and hiked up his trousers.

"You've more on the ball than all of them put together. So, you're a little older. Look at it this way; you've a lot more experience. Stop worrying; you'll do just fine." He ran his fingers through his hair and adjusted his cap.

"You know what your trouble is, don't you, Scotty?"

"What's that?" He looked surprised.

"You're prejudiced," she said, smiling.

"And, you know something?" he countered. "You're right. And, you know something else?" he offered. "I enjoy my prejudices!"

Tracy tossed her auburn curls and laughed. "You're great for my ego. But, I guess it was a good run, eh?" She was fishing—looking for a little confirmation.

"Good? It was bloody fantastic, lass. You were born to the saddle." He looked toward the sky and shivered a bit. "Umm, still a bit nippy," he said and zipped up his jacket. "C'mon, I'll buy you a cup of coffee and a doughnut. You deserve it . . . as soon as I see that Harry takes care of Becket." Scotty knew the groom was roaming around somewhere. He always turned up; practically lived at the track, always there early and the last to leave at night. Scotty often wondered if he ever did leave—or if he slept in one of the stables. Harry was one of the track's enigmas.

Tracy was replying to his invitation. "No, thanks, especially, the doughnut—too many calories. Besides, I think I'd like to walk around the track by myself a little, Scotty—watch the sun come up."

Scotty was disappointed; he loved her company, but he said nonchalantly, "Suit yourself, lass. You know where I'll be—over at the coffee wagon."

Tracy shoved her cap and gloves in the pockets of her leather jacket and shook her hair loose about her. "I love this time of day." She raised her arms to the sky. "I just feel like walking."

Leaning next to a tree, hidden in the shadows near the stables, a tall, muscular figure watched, remembering another young girl who loved to ride horses. She, too, had been slim and full of life, but her hair had been golden and he had loved her with all his heart. She was rich, pampered, and a little spoiled. She broke his heart and she was dead. The tall, silent figure let a sigh escape as painful memories came tumbling back. "Why couldn't it have worked?"

He had wanted a wonderful life with his beautiful bride. She was so full of energy, outgoing, and gregarious. Now, after all this time, he could still hear her haunting, contagious laugh. He squeezed his eyes shut, trying to erase her memory, but only succeeded in making the image sharper. Petite and beautiful, she had had a bewitching smile that still plagued his dreams. He put his hands in his pockets and pushed himself from the tree. Somehow this fiery redhead astride her horse had stirred the memories yet again, made them even more painful. Now, reliving the old hurt, he knew he had blamed a horse for her death, but had he been equally guilty? Maybe if he had tried to understand Vivian—had been a little more patient and let her be the free-spirited girl she truly was she'd still be alive. He had tried to force her to settle down, live life the way he thought it should be lived. That had been the beginning of the end of their marriage. But all the hypotheses and feelings of guilt weren't going to bring her back. He shook himself mentally. And, all his newly acquired wealth—the horses, the property—had been hers, and he was still uncomfortable with it.

He shifted his weight from one foot to the other and recalled how by the end of the first year all Vivian's attention had been focused on her horses and their upkeep. He had begun to feel as if he were in competition with them. At first it was the horses, but then her interest shifted to other men.

The fact was they had never really known each other that well. They had met at a Chesapeake Bay marina, where he had been working on a new boat. He fell head over heels in love with her; there was a hasty marriage and a honeymoon on the French Riviera. The honeymoon lasted for one year. He wasn't used to all the leisure time and partying. He and his father had had a small houseboat, and after his father's death, he had supported himself by working on boats owned by wealthy men. He appreciated the value of the dollar.

He wanted children desperately, and he knew that someday, she would, too, but she was still so young. She had time, and he wasn't going to push her. In the meantime, they had settled down to become total strangers. He loved to sail; she loved to ride. He had a workshop made for himself in an old guest house on the grounds. Slowly, they drifted, the chasm growing wider each day.

It was a rainy day when she rode her horse toward the shelter of the gazebo. The horse lost its footing and tossed her. She never regained consciousness. Quietly and desperately, the bereaved, depressed husband tried to forget. He never wanted her money; but he had no choice—it was his—that and the damned horses! Now, with the worst behind him, he stared at the figure who succeeded in pushing the whole painful past into the present.

A slight breeze whipped through the trees, rustling the leaves, interrupting his reverie. He took a few steps and moved closer.

"You ride just like a man"—the deep resonant voice called out—"and that filly can run."

Tracy, startled, turned too quickly and almost fell off the back of the bench on which she had been sitting. She leaped from the bench and whirled to meet the massive stranger. She hesitated in the dim morning light. His tall frame was silhouetted by a pink and yellow sky, and shadows crossed the sun-tanned face, with the deep-set, sad, brown eyes; but he smiled. He looked lean and tired, this man who had been watching her. What could he want, Tracy asked herself. Probably just some hot tips on the next day's races. As he walked closer to her, Tracy stared. He wasn't the stranger she had first taken him to be. The rugged face was familiar. It took her a moment to place him, but then she knew with utter certainty who this man was. And he was every bit as handsome as he'd been years ago.

"Oh," she cried, "I didn't see you—you frightened me. I'm . . ."

"I'm sorry—I didn't mean to . . ." He smiled again and the creases crinkled around his eyes. The steady stare never left her for an instant. He examined her from her polished black riding boots to her beige jodhpurs to the tucked-in shirt and black leather jacket. Lastly, he looked at her beautiful chiseled features and thick auburn hair. Her emerald eyes, Mark Flanagan found seductive. He extended his hand in the gesture of introduction. "I'm Mark Flanagan . . ."

"Oh, I know," Tracy said as she clasped his firm grip. She strained her neck and looked him squarely in the eyes.

"You know? I'm sorry—you have me at a disadvantage," he said so formally that Tracy had to smile.

"I'm Tracy Morgan; I met you years ago at my dad's stables. You came several times to buy horses with your wife . . ." Immediately, she could see his body tense; the muscular arms tighten beneath his sweater.

"Oh, I'm sorry," she continued. But all she could remember was the familiar, athletic figure who had first aroused her teen-age emotions, and stirred the passions of a young girl. But, looking at him now, she was startled to find the same gut feeling returning.

"It's all right," he said, but the easy manner and smile disappeared from his handsome face. Then, just as quickly, he smiled and jammed his hands into his pockets. A look of recognition appeared in his eyes and he threw his head back. "Tracy? Not old Bull Morgan's skinny, freckle-faced daughter?" He started to laugh. "I can't believe it . . ."

"Believe it, trust me," she said slightly acerbically. She stretched in an attempt to appear taller. Tracy decided subtlety was not one of this man's finer points, nor diplomacy for that matter. Damn him, she thought angrily—"skinny and freckle-faced" . . .

He continued, lost in his discovery. "Well, well, I wouldn't have guessed it . . ."

"Before you ask me what happened, I'll help you out. She's all grown up!" Tracy said rather haughtily and craned her neck in an unsuccessful attempt to meet him at eye level. He still towered over her. He must have been six feet two inches tall. But it was a welcomed change to look up—as opposed to down—as she had to so often do with

17

the other jockeys. The thought brought a smile to her face.

"Well, whatever's made you smile, I'm happy to see it. For a moment I thought you were angry with me." He paused. "And yes, indeed, young lady, you certainly are all grown up!"

Tracy thought she detected a note of interest in the resonant voice. She blushed right down to her toes. "To the first part of your statement, yes, I'm smiling, but I'm afraid it's a private joke; as to the second, about my being angry—I guess my Irish flares up whenever anyone mentions my freckles. Besides," she continued in a teasing voice, "you probably were never aware, but years ago I had a crush on you. You must realize," she said with a laugh, "you were one of the first males who crossed our threshold who wasn't a trainer, groom, or a jockey. In fact, next to my father, you were practically the first *tall* male I had ever laid eyes on. I was beginning to feel that I was in the world of little people. Why, when I was a kid I thought of you as my knight in shining armor!"

He laughed, and to Tracy's delight he seemed actually to blush. He turned toward the jockey's circle, where the finely manicured hedges were being touched by the rays from the first strong sunlight and said, "Would you like to walk a little, Tracy? I've checked on the horses I came to see and now I'm headed for my car. This time of day— early morning—is my favorite time. It's so clean and peaceful."

"Yes, yes, I would," she said eagerly—maybe a bit too enthusiastically. She loved this time of day, too, and she was not one to hide her emotions very well. Her father had told her she wore her heart on her sleeve, and when she grimaced at the use of

18

the cheap cliché, he reminded her of the first time they had lost a foal and she sat up in the stall the entire night while the poor animal lay on its side, moaning. They had told Tracy it wouldn't live till the morning, but she wouldn't listen; she'd been adamant. She stayed the whole night and talked to the little creature, trying to make it comfortable while she covered it with a blanket and continually wiped the perspiring hide with a cool cloth. She talked to it—begged it not to die—but the infection had spread and the animal had been too weak. The next morning, after it had died, she stayed in her room and cried and refused to go to school.

Her father had tried to explain that this was part of the horse business, that this foal hadn't been the first or the last to die, and she must start to accept the unpleasantries in life. But Tracy wouldn't listen, and her father had finally sighed and allowed her to stay by herself for the day and mourn, but only for one day. The next day he drove her to school and made no further mention of it. When she alighted from the car, her father had leaned over and kissed her and said, "That's my girl." She'd still been hurting, but she was proud of herself for her father's acknowledgment.

"Have I lost you, Tracy?" the tall figure asked quietly.

"Oh, I'm sorry, I was daydreaming . . ."

"More private thoughts, about knights in shining armor?" He leaned over and smiled at her. He made her feel about twelve years old.

"No," she answered, and for the first time in a long time, Tracy was uncomfortable. There was an aura about him that made her feel strangely giddy. She thought she was in command of her emotions,

19

but this man kept proving her wrong. Suddenly, she felt shy and awkward. She cleared her throat and looked at her hands nervously, and continued. "It was something you said that triggered an old memory; but don't worry; I've outgrown my crush long ago. I've been truly in love for years now!"

Now it was he who looked bewildered. "Love?" He cocked his head and looked at her, making her feel uneasy.

"Well, it actually started long before my teens . . ." She paused. Damn him, I wish he wouldn't look at me like that; I feel so foolish. She looked up and faced him squarely, "May I call you Mark?"

"That's my name." He smiled indulgently.

She reddened. "Yes, I know, and I know you're going to laugh, but I was almost going to call you Mr. Flanagan."

"Only if you're talking about my father," he said and laughed. "I'm only thirty-seven; I hope I haven't aged that drastically."

No, no, Tracy wanted to scream, you're gorgeous. Why was she saying all the wrong things? She felt tongue-tied. His voice sent tremors through her, and those eyes did drastic things to her nervous system.

"Tracy," he interjected before she could say anything, "you're good medicine for me. I haven't had such a good laugh in a long time."

"I hope it's not at my expense, Mark," she said emphatically. She had the decided feeling he was laughing *at* her, and she didn't like it. But when he turned, pushed his fingers through his hair, and smiled, she melted.

"Well, you'll have to blame my father for my good manners, Mark. He always said he didn't possess them, so his kid would. 'You'll go to college and like it, or I'll be damned,' he told me." She had her hands on her hips, her feet spread apart, and she was rocking back and forth, emulating the familiar stance of her impressive father.

He laughed. "You do a great imitation of your father." Then he stopped walking and looked at her with the deepest, most intense eyes she had ever seen. She was lost in them; her heart was pounding, and she was sure he could hear the thumping. The way he stared down at her made her want to reach up and make sure her blouse was fully buttoned. What a young, impressionable fool he made her feel. But he had resumed talking, and she had to concentrate to make sense of his words.

"Of course I'm not laughing at you, Tracy. It's refreshing to find someone who considers other's feelings . . ." And then he stopped. "But, come on, you were going to tell me of this great love that's possessed you all these years. I'm all ears. Don't leave me hanging; I can't stand mysteries."

Sparked by his interest, she cleared her throat and continued. "Well, it wasn't any two-legged creature that had captured my fancy." She looked at him from the corner of her eye. Some of her confidence was returning since he seemed sincerely interested in her story, and she was about to discuss her favorite subject. She smiled at him coquettishly. "It was one of the four-legged variety. By the time I was two, I was in the saddle, and it was a love affair that began with the first whinny. I was captivated. I'd ride through my father's estate as if I were on the wings of Pegasus." Tracy smiled beguilingly, aware that he was studying her. She tucked in her shirt and ran her fingers through her long hair, all the while kicking at pebbles with her boot. "I love horses; they're my life. Now you know"—she tossed her head back, laughing,—"of my torrid romance. That's why I was out so early this morning. I was running Becket through her paces."

She paused and ran her tongue over her lips, moistening them, and shielded her eyes with her hand as she looked up at him, squinting. He did not interrupt, but looked at her, a tiny smile curling his lips.

"You see," she continued, "I'll ride my first mount in a few days and I'm just overjoyed and nervous, all at the same time. But Becket is such a beauty; you should see her take the hurdles, and even in the wet—"

"Hold on, hold on, I'm convinced!" he exclaimed and raised his hands in mock surrender. He turned slowly toward her and his eyes were sad because he was thinking of another beautiful woman who loved horses—but probably in a different way—more of an ostentatious display than a true caring, he thought. His eyes misted, nonetheless. He cleared his throat and resumed walking, taking her by the arm as they skirted a deep chipmunk's hole in the grass.

His grip on her arm was strong but tender, and Tracy, in spite of the cold, felt warm all over. She could tell from his expression that he was in torment. But what could she say? How could she comfort him? He released her arm, and to dispel the mood she spoke next with a lilting tone to her voice, as if she never noticed the hidden hurt in the eyes.

"So you see, Mark, it's important to me—this first, true, all-consuming love. In two days I ride my first mount, Becket. And I'm a nervous wreck.

I have to make up for lost time. In a lot of ways I'm way behind the other apprentice jockeys; they're so much younger than . . ."

"You're only a young girl yourself . . ."

"I am not." She put her hands on her hips and drew in a deep breath, straightening up her slim, firm body. "I'm twenty-five and that's not young . . ." She was obviously upset.

"Oh, yes, it is, my girl. Oh, yes, it is, especially when you're thirty-seven . . ."

"But that's *young*," she said, "for a man."

He laughed heartily. "Tracy, you're a delight. Anyway, what I meant is that you don't look all those tragic twenty-five years. You look eons younger."

"It's all this clean living." Her head was down and she was kicking the dirt with her boot, with her unruly hair hanging down, hiding her face. Tracy felt herself diminishing in stature and age. She had started out at twelve; she was now about eight. Why did he have that effect on her?

He leaned over and patted her head. She had an uncontrollable urge to punch him, or at least pull his hand away. That's what her father always did to her, especially when he thought he had the better of her. It was patronizing and she didn't like it. She was touchy about a lot of things these days, she reflected.

He looked at his watch. "Well, as much as I've enjoyed our talk, I'm sorry but I've an appointment." He paused and added quietly, as if he weren't sure he should mention it. "But, I wish you the best of luck, my fiery redhead, or as they say in show business, break a leg—"

She interrupted quickly. "I don't think that's a good phrase for a prospective jockey."

23

"No, I suppose not. Bad choice," he said. "Anyway," he looked at her and gave her a delightful, crooked smile, "I'll see you soon."

When? When? she demanded silently. Her heart was pounding, and she had to take a deep breath before she spoke. Very casually, she returned, "I have to run, too. Good-bye, Mark."

He gave her a long look. "Good-bye seems so final. I have the feeling we'll be seeing more of each other." He turned, started to walk, then stopped abruptly. Her heart skipped. He called over his shoulder, "Oh, and maybe next time we meet, you'll tell me why they refer to your father as Bull."

She yelled back. "You can look at him and *still* ask that question?"

He laughed, waved, and walked toward the curb where a Lincoln Continental was parked. She watched him get in and pull away. She watched till the car was out of sight.

Tracy's story to Mark was only partly true. She had always loved her horses, but since she was fifteen and had for the first time seen Mark Flanagan at her father's estate, she never forgot him. She was captivated. While most girls that age already had three crushes behind them, Tracy's interests had been directed toward her horses and training. Mark Flanagan was the first to puncture her busy, private world. She remembered him as the first to stimulate and arouse her. Besides her horses, another interest had surfaced; her appetite was whetted. It was a young girl's fantasy, but he became an obsession, and the tall, dark stranger occupied her waking dreams as well as her dreams at night.

But now he was no longer inaccessible, unattain-

24

able. He was real. She knew of his wife's death and she hated herself for feeling no remorse. The brief contact she had had with him had sent her emotions into a turmoil.

Tracy expelled a deep breath. She was nervous. She put her hands in her back pockets and stared after him. She could handle her horses with no trouble—but this was different.

Once before, years ago, her concentration had been broken with the entrance of this tall, disturbing figure; but that was just infatuation—hero worship. Now, on the brink of her new career, again this enigma had materialized out of the cool, misty morning; however, this scenario was different. She was no longer the starry-eyed youngster, she was a grown woman, a grown woman with emotions, passions—and when it came to Mark Flanagan, passions that were easily aroused. He disturbed and thrilled her all at the same time. Tracy was experiencing feelings that were new to her.

She watched the dust raised by his car settle, and she turned, fingering the lucky charm she was wearing. It had been her mother's, who died when Tracy was twelve. It was a gold brooch with an embossed head of Queen Nefertiti on it. Tracy, for the first time in a long while, thought of her dead mother and the brooch she had left her. She fingered it affectionately and whispered as she headed for the stables, "Mom, help me; I need your strength."

CHAPTER TWO

It began as a brisk, chilly day for September, but by noon the sun had warmed the track considerably, and green grass was everywhere. It had rained heavily the day before and the smell of fresh-cut grass filled the air. There was no breeze —an asset to any race—and there was an air of euphoria to the group that buzzed around Tracy.

Old Gus, the assistant trainer, who had been with her father since they left Ireland, was watching Harry, the itinerant groom, who whistled as he tightened the bandages around Becket's ankles. Gus had been head trainer for years, but his legs bothered him too much, so he stepped down to become the assistant to Scotty, the younger man. Gus had worked hard all his life and he needed to slow down. But, like Bull Morgan, he never really did. He just changed titles with Scotty, and there were no hard feelings.

"Tighter, m' boy, tighter," Gus instructed young Harry.

"Okay, Gus, okay, but she's gotta have some give."

"Yes, yes, I know; it's just that we want everythin' to go right for Tracy today. She's as nervous as a cat." And Harry smiled up at him. Gus was the one who was acting like an expectant father.

Gus looked over at the slim, auburn-haired beauty, who was talking to old Bull. Just like her mother, Gus reflected, beautiful, tough, and determined. And she knew her horses as well as did people twice her age. Bull Morgan was giving her last-minute instructions, together with Scotty. Her agent, a smaller, squatter version of Bull, Ken Watson, stood alongside.

"Ah, if only Margie Morgan were here to see this," he said with a sigh. Gus Walker was small and wiry with a full mane of white, coarse hair. He was easygoing, trustworthy, and self-effacing. Many a wealthy horse-owner had tried to ply him away from the Bull, such was his reputation, but he had remained steadfast. He had been a jockey in Ireland for more years than he cared to remember, but he tore both knee cartilages in an accident and the strength had never returned to his legs, and he had never ridden again. He helped Cornelius "Bull" Morgan build his empire. They went way back. He smiled as he watched Morgan giving instructions to everyone in sight. Bull Morgan was tall and beefy, possessed a massive chest, with not the wisp of a hair left to disturb his bald pate, ruddy-faced, with a cigar constantly in evidence, explosive, irascible—but the best breeder of horses Gus had ever known. He was also Gus's best friend. They were the antithesis of each other, and had they been on the stage in one of Shakespeare's productions, they would have been perfect foils for one another. They fought constantly and shared a comradery that only fighting-friends can. There were no hatreds, no diabolical plots, no secrets. They just were!

"Hey, Gus," Morgan yelled, "everything all right with Becket?"

"Do ya doubt me abilities, Bull?" Every once in a while he'd revert to his Irish brogue for effect. But Gus Walker was no fool. He was a voracious reader, but kept his ideas and philosophies to himself—unless, of course, a bottle of good bourbon was opened—then he'd become the loquacious leprechaun.

"No, no, you old cronie. I'm just concerned for my little girl."

Tracy smiled, listening to the two men banter; she was so happy, caught up in the atmosphere of her first race. It was hot and hectic, but she loved it. The cacophony of noises was music to her ears. It was alive—electric. She was ecstatic, all her thoughts centered around her first mount. It was finally happening. Then, craning her neck to watch all the other horses being walked to their stalls, she saw him. Silent and staring—a face in the crowd. But he didn't notice her. She stepped on tiptoe and swallowed.

"What are you looking for, lass?" Scotty called as he adjusted Becket's blanket and brushed the horse's mane.

"Oh, nothing, nothing—just looking at that crowd. What a mob." She dropped back from her strained position and began tucking her hair atop her head. Mark's presence made her all the more anxious.

"The crowd makes it all worthwhile, kid; by the way"—Scotty shot her a concerned look—"how's your stomach, Trace?"

"My stomach?" She turned quickly. "What do you mean, 'how's my stomach'?" she asked defensively.

"Slow down, kid; I only asked 'cause you said it was upset yesterday."

28

"Oh, that—just something I ate, I suppose." Or something I didn't eat, she thought. Lately, she was having a terrible time keeping her weight down, and she wanted to make sure she weighed in at her apprentice's weight of 104 pounds. Tossing off unpleasant thoughts, she shrugged and patted her slim hips. She'd be all right; besides, it was a beautiful day. The colorful crowds, the excitement, and the roaming banjo players all added to the circus atmosphere. She loved it. It was in her blood, and Belmont was her favorite track. She felt lucky here. And, to herself she admitted, she felt doubly excited knowing Mark was in the stands. She flushed thinking of him.

Someone patted her head and she whirled. "Damn," she whispered.

"Take it easy, girl, it's only your old pa." He ran his hand over his bald head.

"Oh, Pop, I'm sorry. I just feel like I'm going to explode."

"Nonsense, baby, you're just nervous, which is natural and good. It gets all the adrenaline flowing. Besides, you've been through this a thousand times. You're the best. Today it just becomes official."

"Finally." She lowered her voice. "Don't forget, Dad, it's because of you I'm starting out at twenty-five. You were the one who made me go to college, as well as work on your books and learn the administrative end of the business. Because of you I trained, trained, trained . . ."

"So that when I leave this lowly life and my business to you, no charlatan will come in and take it from you. You've a good head. You won't be able to ride forever; you've got to have knowledge and books . . ."

He was flailing the air with his cigar, and she knew everything he said was true. She put her arms around him and said, "I know, I know. You only want what's best for me."

"You're right." He pushed her away and looked at her at arm's length. "Ah, you're the spittin' image of your mother. She'd be proud of you today."

Tracy fingered her medallion. "You're a con artist, you old Bull," she said with a wink.

"Here, here, a little respect for the old man."

"That'll be the day you consider yourself old. I see you still spying the ladies."

"Well, I never . . ." and he grabbed her to him again. It was empty chatter, but they both knew it eased the tension. She looked over his shoulder, and then she saw him! He was walking near the rail that separated the spectators from the racing personnel, where they could observe the horses before they circled and entered the track. The veteran horse players liked to see how their choices reacted while being groomed and saddled before entering the track.

As her father held her, she began squirming; she couldn't stand still. He leaned back and took her by the shoulders. "Hey, missy, settle down . . ."

"Sorry, Pop. I told you I'm nothing but a bundle of nerves. Those little pins and needles are running up and down me legs." She winked at him and patted his bald head. Over his shoulder, she could see Mark make a good luck sign to her, and she returned the wave. Her father turned to see who it was.

"Well, I'll be . . . it's Mark Flanagan. I didn't know he was back; it's about time." And the hefty Irishman brandished his cigar in Mark's direction.

Tracy's heart was working overtime. "Well, I'd

better go and get ready, Pop." She looked away from Mark; she was nervous enough.

"Oh, right, honey. Have Scotty take you and weigh you in—you'll have plenty of time till the next race. Race number three—my lucky number. You'll do just fine, my colleen." Then he turned from her and yelled to Scotty. "Hey, Scot, let's get my girl saddled up!" Scotty was there in a shot.

"C'mon, lass, let's get you baptized."

"Okay, Scotty." She smiled. But when she looked over her shoulder, the face in the crowd had disappeared.

"Hey, smile, Trace. We've got a race to win."

She smiled wanly and followed him to the changing room.

"Riders up!" the familiar voice called and all the jockeys were given a foot up by their grooms. They paraded around the Walking Ring before filing out onto the track.

Tracy was in green-and-white silks, her favorite colors, and she sat her horse proudly. Out of the corner of her eye she saw her father and his entourage, but not Mark. They were waving and cheering as she just rode quietly, being guided toward the track by the Outrider. There were exclamations of encouragement to favorite riders and denigrating ones to those who weren't bringing in the money for the big spenders. But it was all in fun and part of the game. Tracy focused straight ahead and Scotty mumbled to her, "You look the best of the lot, lass."

She said nothing as her sweaty palms held the reins. Then as they turned the corner hedge where the familiar bugler with the black cap and red-and-white outfit announced that the horses were on the track, a thrill soared through Tracy.

31

This was it! They rode among cheers and jeers for 100 feet, then turned back and headed for the starting gate. She passed the stands and looked in the owners' boxes. There he was, Mark Flanagan, handsome and remote. She fingered her mother's Nefertiti brooch.

She was jerked out of her reverie as the microphone clicked.

"*The horses are in the gate . . .* And *they're off!*"

"*And, it's Majestic in the lead, but coming on fast is Becket,*" the announcer was screaming. "*Now they're in the stretch.*" The entire track was on its feet. "*Now they're neck and neck, and Becket takes the lead, ladies and gentlemen. And, it's Becket to the finish by a length. And, there she stands in the saddle, ladies and gentlemen, Tracy Morgan, an apprentice and her first ride!*"

There were screams from the stands, and Tracy stood rigid in the stirrups as Becket and the other horses went over the finish line. Tears streamed down her face as she turned the horse and headed toward the Winner's Circle. Her father, Scotty, Gus, Ken, Harry—they were all running toward her, but she had eyes only for a tall figure who stood in his box with an enigmatic smile on his face.

"But you must join us," Bull Morgan was saying. "We're having a celebration dinner in a little restaurant near home." He had his arm around his daughter and pointed his cigar in the direction of the parkway. "We'll meet you at Alex's Pier 92 at 7:30. We won't take no for an answer. You're no stranger," he was saying to Mark Flanagan. "C'mon, boy, join us. There'll only be eight or ten." He looked at his daughter, whose long tresses were pushed back, the perspiration dampening the curls around her forehead. Her cheeks were flushed and she felt ten feet tall.

"C'mon, Tracy, ask Mark to join us."

Tracy's body was still heaving in wondrous gasps. "Well, maybe Mark has some other plans."

Mark looked at the slender jockey, an inexplicable feeling of pride suffusing him. "No, no, as a matter of fact, I don't. I just didn't want to intrude on a family . . ."

"What family? These are all friends," Morgan said, extending his free arm to encompass his stable full of helpers.

"We'd like to have you, Mark," Tracy said rather formally. She was almost hoping he'd decline. Here on her home ground—her own turf—she felt secure. Outside of these surroundings, she was still uncertain, vulnerable.

"How can I refuse the winner's request?" He winked. "I'll meet you at 7:30." He turned to Tracy and extended his hand. "May I shake the hand of the lovely winner?" Her father released her and turned to Gus and yelled, "Make sure Harry walks Becket till she's good and cooled down, and—"

"You telling me my job, Bull?" Gus yelled back.

"Oh, for Pete's sake, Gus," he said and walked over toward Becket's stall.

Mark still held Tracy's hand. "You have quite a grip for a . . . for a lady jockey."

His strong hand over hers made her pulse quicken and she felt the blood rushing to her face. She was certain she was flushed, and she answered in a husky voice.

"A strong grip is important to our trade . . ."

33

She paused, giving her voice time to return to normal. "Did you enjoy the race?"

"Your father must be very proud," he said, avoiding her question.

"That's not what I asked you." She looked up into the deep, intense eyes.

"You, my young lady, ride like a trooper. I'm happy for you if that's what you want."

"Yes, it's *exactly* what I want." She felt as if he were holding back. She expected a more enthusiastic reaction to her triumph. It had been her first race and she had won. That was a fait accompli. She was bursting with pride. The photographers had snapped her picture, and she'd be written up in the Sports pages of all the newspapers the next day. Why did he seem to resent her success?

He looked down at her and said, "It's a dangerous business; you could get hurt . . ."

"Just as dangerous as driving a car or sailing a boat."

"Okay, okay, touché. If it's what you want, then I'm happy for you."

"Trace, c'mon," Scotty was yelling. "Some chaps want a few more pictures."

"Well, the celebrity must appease her public. I'll see you at dinner."

"Yes, yes." Her heart was racing. And, he turned and left and she ran to join her friends. She was so happy, she thought she'd burst.

There was music with dinner and everybody overate and overdrank, except Tracy. She picked at some salad and no one seemed to notice but Mark. Alex, the old Greek who owned the place and who had known the Morgan family for years, played a melody just for Tracy on his guitar. It was a gay and foot-stomping number, and all ended up cheering and raising their glasses.

Mark leaned across the table, and through the din of voices and music, said to Tracy, "How about a stroll outside? I don't think they'll miss us much." He pointed to Gus and her father, who were doing an Irish jig while the rest clapped and kept time with the music.

"I'd love it," she shouted back.

They slipped out the back door into a garden filled with trees and bushes. The grounds sloped down toward the water and there was a warm breeze rustling the leaves of the trees. Lights from small boats danced across the Long Island Sound.

"Walk down to the water," he said with a rakish smile, "my little winner?"

"Not so little, I'm afraid. I'm tall by jockey's standards."

"Yes, but so slim."

"It's all part of the . . ."

". . . trade," he finished for her. They both laughed.

The green hill was slippery with the evening's dew, and as they sauntered down casually, Tracy slipped on the incline, and Mark quickly grabbed her about the waist.

"Oh," she gasped. She could feel his sinewy muscles as his arms surrounded her. The moon ducked behind a cloud, and they were in darkness with only the reflection from the tiny boats' lights.

"I . . . I guess I'm not as steady on my feet as I am on a horse," she said huskily. His arms circled her slim waist and he drew her nearer to him.

"Are you okay now?" His voice was deep and just above a whisper. He was breathing heavily.

"Yes, yes . . ." she said as their eyes locked.

35

Mark didn't remove his hand from her waist; instead, his arm remained encircled around it, and he led her down the path slowly, saying nothing. Tracy's emotions were at their peak and her head was a mass of confusion. Then, his strong hand took hers and he turned to face her. The moon peeked from behind the clouds and a yellow light danced across his tanned face; she was lost in his deep, soul-searching eyes. And for a brief moment she thought he was going to kiss her. How she wished with all her being that he would! Instead, he turned away and led her by the hand along the water's edge, where the only sound was the rhythmic slapping of the waves against tiny boats. His hand was gentle but firm and his fingers played nervously with her wrist. Tracy knew her feelings were ridiculous. She hardly knew the man and hadn't seen him in years, but still, she wanted that sensuous mouth on hers. She knew he wouldn't; the moment had passed, and she felt that he was going to be sensible for both of them. But something had passed between them at that brief moment—an electricity, that was almost tangible. She wanted to reach up and pull him to her. She wanted to taste that mouth. She ached for him. And as they walked in silence, communicating while saying nothing, the mood was dispelled by the sound of music and laughter drifting down from the patio. Some of the party was moving outside.

He continued to hold her hand firmly and they turned in the direction of the music and noise as a gentle breeze brushed over them. Tracy, however, was still on fire with her inner excitement.

Voices were calling them back. "Hey, Tracy, where are you?" It was Scotty.

36

"Just taking a walk," she yelled back, trying to keep her voice casual and light. "It was so hot in there."

Mark looked at her, smiled, and released her hand. They turned toward the restaurant and started to climb the incline.

"Well, c'mon, we're goin'—your father's gettin' the car." There was just a twinge of annoyance to the Scot's voice.

"Okay, I'll be right there."

"Well, snap it up; you've got some workouts to do tomorrow. We can't be too late. *Some* of us have to work for our money!"

Of course, the remark was meant for Mark, and Tracy just said quietly, "He's just a little drunk. Too much wine . . ."

"Don't worry about me, I'm pretty thick-skinned." He smiled at her. Her knees again went to water.

As the others filed inside the restaurant, boisterously, he cleared his throat and found solace in his brown shoes.

"Tracy . . . I . . ." he paused. Mark Flanagan was suddenly tripping over himself. Words had somehow failed him. He was definitely drawn to this little bundle of energy, and he had all he could do tonight to keep his hands off her, but he just wasn't ready for any commitments and wouldn't be for a long time. But Tracy was so overwhelmed with the day's winnings and the evening's excitement that she never saw the concern in his eyes. She just saw him—tall, strong, virile—and she knew he cared for her. She could feel it. She didn't want to think past that as she waited for him to finish.

They climbed the little hill and he said abruptly,

"I . . . well, I'd like to take you to Mitchell's for dinner on Friday night."

"Oh, I can't Friday; I'm riding on Saturday, so I'll have to work out and rest."

He looked disappointed, Tracy thought, and she was glad. "But, Saturday night would be all right," she said with a smile.

"Good, I'll pick you up at 7:00." Then, as they reached the patio, he added, "It'll give us a chance to become better acquainted."

"I hope so," she said slowly, and she turned her head coquettishly, allowing her long tresses to frame the angular face.

"C'mon, Tracy"—a gruff voice came from inside —"we're waiting."

"You'd better hurry; your public awaits. Till Saturday, Sprite."

"Sprite?" She turned, questioningly. "Aren't I a little too big to be a sprite?"

"Not really. Besides, it also means, mischievous, devilish—and I see both those qualities in you."

"Whatever," she told him, and walked through the restaurant toward the front door where her friends waited for her. All the men were slightly tipsy as they were saying good night to Alex. It was a comical sight. She laughed at the scene.

And then it hit her; the pain in her stomach. It was really more of a pang than a pain—a pang of hunger. But she knew the feeling would pass. It always did. Besides, she was too happy.

"Hey, I've been looking for you guys all over," she yelled. "Where've you been? I've got to get home." They turned and watched the slim body race toward them.

"Bloody fresh kid," Bull yelled. But he smiled. "Just like her mother."

And then they all piled into the cars. Gus sat beside her with his arm around her, proud as if she were his own daughter. She rested her head on his shoulder and closed her eyes, seeing that strong, handsome face before her. But the gnawing pain inside the empty hollow was not receding—she was very hungry and had hardly eaten a thing. I could eat a bull, she thought, and laughed to herself at the pun. As the car drove on, she dozed with her slim fingers pressed against her stomach.

CHAPTER THREE

Tracy dressed carefully for her Saturday night date. She brushed her hair back from her face and arranged it in an old Gibson Girl style. It afforded her that little extra touch of sophistication, she thought, with which she wanted to impress Mark.

His calling her a sprite and telling her she didn't look her twenty-five years bothered Tracy. Well, she'd show him. She slipped on a black sheath that hugged her slim frame and then put on her new Givenchy sling-back heels. Next, she added a wide gold choker that gave her a Victorian look. Tracy clipped on the emerald and gold earrings her father had bought her for her twenty-first birthday. Her green eyes sparkled.

She appraised herself in the mirror. In her high heels she was approximately five feet eight inches. Eat your heart out, Brooke Shields, she thought as she turned this way and that, affecting different poses and feeling very pleased with herself. When she heard a car pull up, she felt like a school girl and rushed to the window to see Mark's Continental pull in front of the house.

She grabbed her black mink jacket, heard the chimes, and ran down the stairs to open the door herself. No one else was at home.

Mark Flanagan stood before her in a navy blue

serge suit, with a light blue-striped shirt, and a muted red silk tie. The tiny gray hairs that crept around the temples did nothing but enhance his good looks. He screamed elegance and masculinity.

The deep-set eyes widened, acknowledging the figure before him. He was properly nonplussed.

Different emotions seemed to play across his face as he looked at her: was it delight or pleasure or amusement? She couldn't tell as a tiny smile crept across the rugged face.

All he said was "My, my . . ."

"Are you always so loquacious?" she said and handed him her fur. Dutifully, he slipped it over her shoulders.

"Shall we go, Cinderella?" he said with a chuckle as they headed toward the car.

"That Continental may turn into a horse if you don't have me home by midnight," she quipped.

"Okay, Sprite, let's go." He opened the car door for her.

They rode to Mitchell's in silence. When they arrived, Tracy noticed how well the grounds were kept and tiny well-appointed lights shone from behind bushes and hedges. There was a touch of quiet class that more ostentatious establishments lacked.

Mark handed the keys to the attendant and guided Tracy to the door. Before they walked through the glass portals, they heard the screech of wheels biting gravel as the attendant searched for an empty spot for the impressive car. Tracy and Mark looked at each other and laughed in unison.

"Happens every time." He smiled. "Maybe

41

someday I'll buy a Volkswagen and see if they can raise a *vroom* from that."

As they entered the restaurant, Mark spoke to the maitre d', who ushered them to their table. Heads turned as Tracy and Mark passed. She felt securely elegant and she wanted so much to impress him.

They slid into a quiet booth and the candlelight from the table played across Tracy's gold, accentuating her beauty.

She knew he was pleased with her. His silence was testament to it. The wine captain took his order and returned with a bottle for Mark's approval. He nodded without even tasting the wine and the waiter filled their glasses. Tracy noticed that he shifted in his seat and looked at the captain nervously. She sensed he was uncomfortable with the wine-tasting ceremony, and she smiled to herself. He suddenly looked like a young boy, dressed up, forced to comply to society's standards, and he was ill at ease. This only endeared him all the more to her, because it was evidence of uncertainty—the first she had seen in him. He had seemed so capable and assured before this that she was happy to witness his slight uneasiness; it made him even more attractive in her eyes.

He raised his glass in a toast. "To the winning lady," he said. Their glasses touched.

"Thank you, kind sir," she said demurely and lowered her eyes. "But yesterday I rode two mounts and only came in third in both; that's . . ."

"Terrific," he finished for her. "Tracy, don't be greedy. At least you were in the money. For a woman to—"

She stopped him abruptly. "Do you think my

42

first win was just beginner's luck? I've worked hard." She paused. "And I'm not sure I like that 'for a woman' business."

"Here we go again," he said, "my feisty friend. I only meant, and *not* in a denigrating manner, that you have so much competition; that you're up against the best, and that you're going to have to accept second and third place once in a while."

She raised her glass. "Well, all right," she said a little uncertainly. "I'll drink to that." She emptied her glass and he refilled it.

"I really didn't get an opportunity to tell you how proud—" But the waiter arrived interrupting him. They ordered steaks and salad. Tracy downed another glass of wine; she was beginning to feel very lightheaded. The wine was affecting her; she had eaten only two apples all day. Then perhaps it was not only the wine, she conceded. Mark's very presence made her feel giddy. And when he spoke, his deep, controlled voice sent shivers up her spine. And when he listened, those powerful dark eyes never left hers. Occasionally, his long, rough fingers would brush over her hand, and she would jump involuntarily. He could be very intense when he spoke and his eyes had a hypnotic effect on her. Sometimes she found her mind wandering, wishing he'd take her outside, gather her up in his arms, and smother her with that full, sensuous mouth.

But, she managed to control herself and after the waiter left, she turned her eyes up to him.

"You were saying," she goaded him playfully.

"Well, with all those people there," he cleared his throat and played with the silver. Perhaps he, too, was nervous, Tracy thought. "Well, I didn't get

43

a chance to really express my admiration . . ." He kept talking.

. . . Express my admiration, Tracy thought. He sounds like he's giving a lecture to a convention of retired morticians.

He saw her smile and added, "I thought you were just great!" He quickly downed his drink.

Tracy realized he had difficulty giving her a compliment, especially when it came to her career. A point to remember, she thought. But she smiled graciously and added, "That's better—I love a man who speaks his mind . . ."

"You sound experienced, young lady."

"Only with horses," she teased.

Their eyes met for a moment and she remembered the other night. Her head was spinning. "Mark, could you please order some Perrier; I think I've had enough wine."

As he turned the waiter arrived with the steaks, and he ordered the Perrier.

"Are you all right, Tracy?" he asked a little concerned.

"Of course." She cut into her steak and ate a tiny piece. The Perrier arrived and she sipped. "Ah, that's better." Then she started to nibble on the celery and carrot sticks.

Mark cut a large piece of meat and looked at her. "Aren't you hungry, Tracy?"

"Oh, yes," she lied. "I just like to take my time." Changing the subject, she said, "Tell me, Mark, what did you do before you inherited the horses and . . ."

"Married into money?" He looked up brusquely.

"No, no," she added quietly. "I just mean, well,

44

what did you do when you were young—I mean younger . . ."

He laughed, putting down his knife and fork. "We always seem to come back to age, don't we?"

Rather than speak, since both feet seemed to be where her mouth should be, she grabbed some celery and sought safety in the chomping of a stalk. She felt a bit flushed.

"It's all right, I know what you mean. Well, unfortunately, I was born into the working class. I said unfortunately because Dad didn't always work. Anyway, I worked my way through college at a local marina and finally received my engineering degree. I found, however, that the market was flooded with aspiring young engineers." He looked up from over his wine; Tracy was all attention. "I was lucky. A man I had done some work for, and who was very wealthy intervened for me. Doors flew open, and yours truly started with a very prestigious industrial engineering corporation. But I guess I just couldn't stand the nine-to-five routine and I left and bummed around the country, always working at different marinas. I loved sailing, and I'm still trying to develop a design for a slimmer, trimmer sailboat—but one to retail at an affordable price. As yet, no luck. I still love to work on boats, and I was good at it. That's how I met Vivian—at Chesapeake Bay . . ." He looked up and Tracy was sitting transfixed, over her cold steak, her chin cupped in her hands, intent upon his every word. "Your steak's getting cold," he added.

"Oh yes, yes." She made a cursory cut into the meat, then looked up. "But go on—go on—I want to learn more about you. You were doing what you wanted," she said vigorously. "I think that's the

45

most important thing in life. And now you have the money to pursue your dream further. You shouldn't stop now."

He looked at her hard when she mentioned the money, but realized she meant no harm. He still felt touchy about the vast amount he had inherited from his wife, as if people were always accusing him of not deserving it.

"But," he interjected, "I've also inherited a string of fifteen horses. This is not exactly my forté; but I do have a good trainer and three assistant trainers, and I'm learning—"

She interrupted. "Well, you can pursue both . . ." She still hadn't touched her steak.

"Hey, slow down, miss. I'm not as ambitious as you are. But, we'll see . . ." He pushed his empty plate aside. "And you, Tracy, what about you? What's your ambition, or perhaps I should say, goal. You've attained your ambition, even though youth has passed you by, and you're over the hill." He smiled a beautiful, crooked smile, and Tracy noticed for the first time that he possessed the most perfect teeth she had ever seen.

"Am I that transparent?" She looked up at him.

He simply continued to smile.

"Why, the Kentucky Derby; I'm going to win the Kentucky Derby!" She placed her elbows on the table, raising her chest triumphantly. It was not a hope or a wish. It was an assertion—a certainty.

He kept looking at her and Tracy realized the wine must have unsettled her more than she realized. She felt very warm, very free—freer than she had in a long while.

Even his dark eyes were smiling now. "Well,

that's certainly decisive enough. When will this great triumph take place?"

"Why, when the Kentucky Derby runs, of course." She looked at him as if he came from another galaxy. "In May."

Again, the tolerant smile. "But which May?"

"This one, Mark. Don't forget, I'm not getting any younger!" And she tossed her head back and laughed. Tracy Morgan, she said to herself, you are slightly tipsy.

"And," she continued, "do you know something else?" She grabbed for the wine and not the Perrier. She filled her glass.

"I think you've had enough wine, Tracy; would you like some coffee?" His eyes came to rest on her unfinished steak.

She ignored his request, sipped the wine, and continued. "You have the most beautiful teeth I've ever seen!" Now she giggled and he joined in the laugh.

"I think you've needed a night out on the town, as they say, for some time, Miss Morgan."

Suddenly she blushed and her hand shot to her flushed cheek. He noticed the slim, strong fingers. "Oh, my goodness, I'm all flushed. I think you're right, Mark; maybe I should have some coffee or something."

He flagged the waiter and ordered coffee. "Dessert?" he asked.

"No, no," she added quickly, her green eyes chastising him. "None for me." She patted her hip playfully.

When the coffee arrived, Tracy took several quick gulps and sat back in the booth. "Oh, that's better." She leaned her head back on the leather cushion. Music was beginning to filter through

47

from the dance floor. She closed her eyes and hummed with the music. Mark slid over in the booth next to her. His hand brushed hers on the seat and her eyes immediately flew open. He picked up his coffee cup and drank; Tracy followed suit.

"Relaxed?" he asked.

"Oh yes, very . . ." she answered, feeling suddenly nervous. She pointed to the coffeepot, indicating she'd like more, and he poured it for her. "Thank you." She sighed. "I love that."

"Coffee?" he asked.

"No, silly, that tune, 'Memories.'" Then she faced him squarely and tipped her head sideways. "I'm sorry, I guess I'm not used to drinking wine—such a regimented life, you know."

"So I've come to understand."

"And," she leaned forward, whispering conspiratorially, "would you do me one little favor?"

"If I can." He leaned over, until their foreheads nearly touched, and looked into her eyes. He fought back an impulse to laugh. She was like a little imp, so vulnerable, so lovely.

"Please," she whispered, "please stop calling me little miss. I feel like an English schoolgirl who's being reprimanded by her nanny for incorrectly holding her teacup."

He laughed aloud. "I'll try to remember." He was tapping his spoon against his saucer and smiling happily, caught up in the mood.

"Good," she whispered. "Now, since we're becoming such good friends, would you do me another little favor?"

"If I possibly can."

"Dance with me." It was not a request, but a command. Their eyes met again.

48

"I'd *love* to dance with you."

He led her to the dance floor, and as he watched her ease past the tables, he could see the muscles in her slim body and the angles of her beautiful shape. The wine, too, had warmed him, and he was determined to follow the night's dictates—whatever they might be.

As he took her in his arms, she faced him and said enthusiastically, "I almost forgot to mention that Pop and my agent have indicated, besides Aqueduct this winter, I'll be flying down to Hialeah and out to Santa Anita to ride. Isn't that exciting?"

"Very," he answered simply. He pulled her to him and glided her around the floor effortlessly. She was weightless and followed his lead perfectly. This young jockey was beginning to crawl beneath his skin, with her openness and honesty. She was different from all the women he had met over the past year. But her ambition and preoccupation with horses reminded him so much of . . .

She was humming in his ear, and then whispered, "You're a very smooth dancer, Mr. Flanagan."

"I was thinking the same of you, Miss Morgan."

They danced for a long while, both enjoying the movement of each other's bodies as they weaved easily to the strains of the music. Tracy was aware of the firm hold he had on her and how he swayed so beautifully with her. He had rhythm, and she fit into his arms perfectly. He gripped her tightly around the waist, leading her in the direction he wanted. Then he pressed his body closer to hers and she felt breathless and lightheaded. She tried to back away, but his grasp was firm and unrelenting. Tracy decided to relax and allowed herself to be led around the floor. She didn't fight, she couldn't fight, and she knew she didn't want to fight.

They were gliding, drifting, and then his tongue began to toy with the tiny wisps of hair around her ear. She swallowed hard, and a tingling sensation ran from the base of her neck down her spinal column. She went limp.

When he finally spoke, his low baritone voice was intoxicating, and she had difficulty focusing. "It's not fair," he whispered, his tongue in her ear, "I've told you a lot about myself, but I know so little about you. Of course," he continued, "I know you're Bull Morgan's daughter."

Tracy swallowed hard; her throat was so dry, and she had a hard time concentrating. "Daughter *and* jockey extraordinaire, if you please." She tried to keep it light, but it wasn't easy. His masculine scent was filling her nostrils and his hand was running up and down her back. His hands were huge and he would spread his palm across her spine as he led her around the floor. The force of it seemed overbearing.

Their lower bodies swayed together in unison. His thighs insinuated themselves against hers and she returned the pressure. Tracy experienced the rough texture of his beard as she brushed her face against his cheek, and his free hand caressed her hair. Tracy was on fire. She attempted to continue the conversation.

"Not much more to say," she said huskily. "You remember me as a skinny—"

But he stopped her with a gentle finger to her lips. "Please, I realize I hit a nerve with that; let's just forget it."

She smiled, settled in his arms, and continued.

"You remember me as a youngster, who ran around her father's estate. Well, even then I wanted to be a jockey. My dad was against it from the start, but as the years passed and I didn't change my mind he began to relent. Finally he said he'd compromise. He'd let me ride if I finished college and learned the business end of my glamorous obsession. So, I trained and studied; ergo, my old-age apprenticeship." Tracy realized she was speaking rapidly, but it was just a cover-up for her inner excitement; she also realized as she was talking that she was toying unconsciously with the back of his neck. She allowed her hand to slowly slide down his back. He was staring intently at her, with just the slightest smile curling the corners of his lips.

The music stopped, and Tracy was almost grateful. "I think they're trying to tell us something." His smile broadened. Was he aware of the effect he was having on her?

She released herself and led the way back to the table. Mark Flanagan's eyes never left her slim waist or her long, beautiful legs as he followed her.

As they angled their way back to their table, Mark also recounted a bit of his youth. "You're not the only one who had to toe the mark. If it hadn't been for my father, I would have turned into a very comfortable beach bum. He made me start college, then after his death, I had no option. I had to work during the day and go to school at night. But at least I worked in the marina, around what I loved—boats." He held her chair for her as she slid in. "So you see, we do have something in common, Tracy. We at least experienced what made us happy."

They sat down. "Shall I order more hot coffee?"

51

"Please," she said.

When the coffee arrived, she was thankful to hold on to something. She was terribly nervous.

"Enough about me, and more about you—what else?"

What else? What else? He was looking at her with such intensity, she wanted to scream. My horses—and now you *again*—that's what else! She lowered her eyes and looked for guidance in her coffee cup. "Well, as I've said, I was practically born on a horse," and she looked up at him. "I don't think you ever met my mom; she died when I was twelve."

"No, I only met your father."

"Well, she really took the time with me; Pop was busy with the business. Anyway, Mom loved horses almost as much as I do. She kept after me, helped me, and she saw my potential—and here I am."

The lights were dimmed further and the music resumed. The candlelight flickered across her face and Mark said quietly, "You miss her, don't you?"

"Yes, yes, I do. She was so understanding and full of life. She probably would have let me ride when I was eighteen, like I wanted. But not Pop; oh, no. It was school and work and train, train, train."

"But it's paid off, Tracy. You're the belle of the ball."

"Oh, sure, today I am, but an audience has a short memory. You have to keep giving them something so they'll come back. So," she turned to him, "you've got to be the best—always on top. You've got to be a winner. That crowd out there is fickle."

"That's a pretty wise philosophy for a young . . . lady."

"That's better than little miss," Tracy said philosophically.

He laughed. "Do you always say what comes to mind?"

"Pretty much," she replied. "I can't see the sense in duplicities, although I won't go out of my way to offend someone. But, on the other hand, I have been accused of having a temper."

"To match that fiery hair," he said. "Which, I might add, the way you've piled it atop your head tonight makes you look years older."

Oh, great, Tracy thought. Here goes ol' Mr. Finesse again. Not gorgeous or attractive, but older. How about sophisticated? she wanted to scream. I spent hours laboring for sophistication. Let's hear it for us sophisticates! But he said nothing more. Tracy would have to settle for older.

He looked away from her and saw the cold steak that she hadn't finished and the waiter hadn't removed. Annoyed, he flagged the waiter and told him to remove the plates. The waiter apologized.

Tracy was swaying her head back and forth to the music.

"Tracy, there is one thing I'd like to mention. You're so thin."

Without opening her eyes, she said, "Have to be, part of the business; must maintain my riding weight."

"That's fine," he said. "I don't mind spending money, but wasting it—that's something else. You didn't eat at all. You had one bite of steak . . ."

She opened her eyes. "You count, too?" She asked a little too sharply. "Would you like me to reimburse you?"

"Watch that temper, miss. It's not as complimentary as your new hairdo."

They stared at each other for an instant and both said simultaneously, "I'm sorry."

Tracy was embarrassed. Her nerves were raw. The wine had worn off and she felt as vulnerable as a two year old. How could she explain her dilemma without sounding foolish? She didn't want to spoil the evening, but it wasn't *all* her fault, she rationalized. She could see he was still annoyed; his lips drawn back in a thin line.

"I'm afraid I wasn't that hungry, Mark. We had company today and I picked too much," she lied.

His expression softened. "It's okay. I shouldn't have mentioned it. As long as you're not starving yourself."

She looked up startled, but quickly smiled. "Who? Bull Morgan's daughter? Never. But I can't afford to overeat either."

"From what I've seen of you there's no chance in that. It's important to eat, Tracy. Besides, I do enjoy company when I dine."

She wished he'd get off the subject; he was getting a little too close to home.

"By the way," he said and brightened. "You were going to tell me the story behind the Bull name. And don't give me that 'you can look at him and still ask that question?' routine. There's always a story behind a name like that."

Tracy was so happy to change the topic of conversation that she smiled sweetly and said she'd tell him, but that it had to be in strictest confidence.

"My lips are sealed."

She leaned forward enthusiastically and her green eyes were afire from the candlelight. "A few years ago, on a cold night, when old Gus uncorked a bourbon bottle, he told me the story." Her eyes were flashing, just like a cat's, Mark thought. She continued. "In County Cork, when Dad was very young, he was coming home from the local pub late at night with Gus and another friend. They decided to cut across a field owned by a man named Halloran when they heard a noise, looked up, and saw Halloran's bull, loose, pawing the ground, and ready to charge them. Gus and the other guy ran, but Pop stood firm. He pulled off his jacket and waved it beside him and yelled, 'Eh, Toro!' Well"—she shifted in her seat—"the bull charged and went for his jacket, and Pop released the jacket so the bull ran blindly with it over his eyes. Then he hightailed it for the safety of the fence, one boot on, one boot off.

"The third guy had taken off, but Gus was perched atop the fence like a leprechaun, and asked, 'Now why in hell did you do that? Who are you tryin' to impress? You could've been killed!'

"'Impress?' said Pop, 'I had no choice, ya damn fool,' he yelled. 'Look at my feet.'

"'Where's your other boot,' asked Gus.

"Pop pointed in the direction of the hole where one lonely boot stood at attention. 'My foot got caught in a woodchuck's hole; I couldn't get it out in time. What else could I do? So, after he charged past me, I pulled my foot out of the boot and ran like hell.'

"So the story was slightly embellished and Cornelius's feat of daring-do was broadcast near and far. Exit Cornelius, enter Bull, and end of story, as related by one drunken Gus."

Mark laughed and rubbed a firm chin. "I love it, and I promise his secret is safe with me."

"It had better be," she said with a laugh, "or you'll fall into disfavor with the 'Horsey' set."

"Ah, 'the sport of kings,'" he said with a sigh. "I promise to honor the masquerade. I'll abide by your rules if you want me to."

"You'd better, Mr. Flanagan." Tracy yawned involuntarily and her hand flew to cover her mouth. "Oh, I'm sorry, Mark . . ."

"I hope it's the hour and not the company; that's not original, I know, but it is getting late. Would you like me to take you home?"

No, I'd like you to take me to *your* home, she thought. Instead, she stretched and said sleepily, "Yes, I'm afraid you'd better. It's pretty late, and I have a busy day tomorrow."

He turned. "You're not racing tomorrow, on Sunday?"

"No, I'm not, but I am scheduled for Monday, so I do have to . . ."

"Work out," he finished.

"Right." She smiled.

"You do love it, don't you?"

"More than anything else," she said without hesitation.

"Yes, yes," he paused rather solemnly. "I can see you do." He turned away from her and motioned for the waiter and the bill.

While he was signing the check, Tracy tucked up the wispy ends of her hair that were starting to unravel from her new hairdo. Damn, she thought, I should have used more hair spray; my sophistication is starting to droop. And, as the waiter returned Mark's American Express card, she thought, he never even said anything about my dress, my total look! Of course, his eyes did seem to speak his approval, but Tracy wanted to hear it. She wanted reassurance.

"All ready?" He was standing and offering his hand.

"Oh, yes, yes. Sorry, I was daydreaming."

As he helped her on with the fur, he squeezed her shoulders and whispered in her ear, "I have competition?"

"What?" She whirled.

"Your daydreams," he said.

"Of course, I told you, and they all have four legs." She turned and headed for the door and Mark followed her body with his eyes—as did most of the other patrons.

The attendant brought the car, and they pulled away quietly, heading into the star-filled night. As they approached Tracy's driveway, Mark pulled over beneath a stand of trees. He rolled down the window to listen to the night sounds. "Pleasant, isn't it?"

"Beautiful," she agreed. Her palms were moist and she rubbed them on her expensive dress.

"I'll be out of town for a couple of days . . ."

"Oh," Tracy said, hardly able to hide her disappointment. So much for her sophistication. "Business?" she asked. Very aggressive, Tracy, she told herself.

"No, some personal affairs; but it'll be settled within a few days." He slid nearer her and played with the top of her slightly wilted two-hour hairdo. "But, next weekend if you're not riding on Sunday . . ."

"No, no," she answered. "As far as I know, I have no mounts on Sunday, but I do have four this week," she announced proudly.

"If I may be allowed to finish?" he teased.

His playing with the crown of her hair was driving her crazy. "Of course."

"Well, you seemed interested in my sailing ventures . . ."

Good grief, he sounds impersonal. Why doesn't he just say it. But, he kept toying with her hair and tiny shivers were maneuvering up and down her spine.

". . . So, I'd like to take you out on ol' *Flossie*."

"*Flossie?* What an odd name."

"Yes, *Flossie*. She's a thirty-two footer and she's a beauty. I have a newer one, but this is my favorite."

"*Flossie.*" Tracy said as if still not believing that could possibly be the name of a boat.

"Yes, *Flossie*—it's not very romantic or original, I admit—but, damn it, she's mine. My first big boat. You horsey people have your Bulls. Well, we sailors have our Flossies!"

"Okay, okay, Mark," Tracy said with a laugh. "And yes, I'd be delighted. Don't get so defensive."

"Well," he said, "it seems I'm surrounded by the world of jocks around here and everything they do is great, but deviate a little in another direction, in an area someone else happens to love, and right away question marks shoot up."

"I didn't mean—"

"And, another thing," he continued, pulling at the pins in her hair.

"What are you doing?" Her hands fluttered to her head like little birds' wings. "Stop!"

"I'm doing something I wanted to do all night. I'm pulling this ridiculous, overly ornate, mid-Victorian hairdo down where it belongs."

"But that took me nearly two hours to do," she objected. "It's very, very . . ."

"False," he said. "You don't hesitate to *say* what

you want. Well, don't hesitate to *be* what you are—a beautiful, natural, fresh-looking woman!"

"Next you'll tell me to get back to basics," she added sarcastically.

He paid her no attention and continued to throw the pins on the front seat, pulling at the thick, wavy mane. Her hair fell to her shoulders, and she tossed her head back and forth with patrician dignity. Tracy was furious. She had spent hours to look her best. She wanted so much to impress him—damn him!

He took her by the shoulders and turned her to him. "Now—you look natural and beautiful; not false and pretentious. I've had all of that that I can handle." He leaned over her heaving body, his deep-set eyes fierce and hungry, and his mouth was on hers in an instant. He was demanding and she went limp, returning his kiss. Her mouth slowly opened allowing his searching tongue to explore her own hot, wet cavern. He was gentle but firm with her. Then his hand slipped beneath her dress and inched up her burning hot thigh. Her muffled moans were stifled by his searing kiss. He pressed her breasts closer to his chest, causing tiny gasps to escape her. And she was screaming inside—love me, Mark, love me—such was the ferocity of his embrace.

Slowly, he released her. His eyes were glassy and he was panting and sweating. He was mumbling something that Tracy couldn't hear. Tracy's breath came in gasps and her breasts were heaving.

"I'll . . . I'll"—he exhaled in a voice hardly audible—"I'll pick you up Sunday at seven o'clock." He didn't wait for a reply, but gunned the engine and jerked the car to an abrupt halt in front of her house. "You'd better jump out quickly, Tracy, I'm only human."

She opened the door, and as she slammed it, yelled at his face that stared straight ahead. "Seven o'clock, Sunday . . ."

But the car bit the gravel and he was gone, pebbles spewing in the driveway.

She toyed with her long hair as she stared after the white car and wondered what it was that had triggered such anger. He didn't seem the type who was prone to unreasonable anger, but then again, how much did she really know of him? Not much.

She looked at the huge house and rubbed her slim arms where he had grabbed her. Bruises were starting to surface. She threw her jacket over her shoulder and headed for the front door. Mark Flanagan was angry at something or someone—and he was filled with passion. She smiled. For that at least she was happy.

As she closed the door behind her, a familiar growl emanated from her stomach. She headed for the kitchen.

For the next few weeks she and Mark saw each other often. He was attentive and came every chance he could to see her ride. She was doing well, receiving acclaim for her riding prowess, and he seemed to take delight in her winnings. But they always seemed to be surrounded by crowds. They were never alone.

The first boat trip aboard *Flossie* had been canceled because an unexpected storm had blown up. Finally, he asked her out again and it was tomorrow. She was thrilled and nervous at the same time. The day was expected to be cloudless, warm, and clear. Tracy was glad for the change of pace and happy at the prospect of being alone with Mark.

"Steady, Sasha," she reprimanded the spunky new filly as she brushed her down. "You're nervous, too, about riding tomorrow, aren't you?" She patted the animal affectionately. "Well, I'm nervous, too. I have a big day coming up tomorrow." The horse whinnied her agreement, and Tracy smiled.

This was her time of reflection—her time to be alone—the only chance she had to think aloud. She needed this time to herself—especially now. Enjoying the new role of the celebrated woman jockey, coupled with the return of the tall, handsome enigma who stirred her to distraction, she was a mass of nerves and excitement. She knew she was wild for him, and here, in the privacy of the stall, alone with Sasha, she could admit it to herself without fear of reprisal. But did he *really* care for her? How did he feel? Her thoughts returned to that night in the car when he kissed her passionately, and she felt good inside.

Tracy remembered his rugged hands in her hair; his hot breath on her neck; the strong, searching fingers climbing up her thighs; and his hungry, sensual mouth on hers—demanding but gentle. How well she remembered—and remembering, she wanted more. She was starved for his embrace.

But Tracy was a little frightened; too much was happening too quickly. She was riding the crest of her new popularity, and she didn't want anything to interfere with that. "But, I want him, too, Sasha," she confided as she brushed the filly more vigorously. "I want him desperately."

CHAPTER FOUR

The sun was rising and highlighting the horizon with its brilliant rays. As they sailed toward it, a huge half circle of pink and yellow cut into the dim gray of the water. Slowly it spread across Long Island Sound; in a few moments the water was awash in the morning's brightness and night was forgotten. A gentle breeze swept across the quiet sea, and Tracy sat on the deck hugging her knees to her chest, watching as Mark hoisted the mainsail.

"You're not going to ask me to attach the jib, or anything like that, are you? I love to sail, but I'm happy to say I don't know the first thing about it."

"No, no," he said and laughed, his back toward her, and Tracy's eyes followed the faded, cut-off jeans that exposed his muscular, sinewy legs. As he hoisted, she tilted her head and noticed that he had ripped out the sleeves of the pale blue T-shirt and a few remaining threads danced over strong, tan muscles. This man was possessed of a powerful body, a body that seemed at home in a blue serge as well as casual sailing clothes. She was becoming warmer, and she knew it was not just from the sun's rays.

He turned toward her, huffing a bit, and smiled. The sun shone on his thick brown hair and emphasized the character lines in his angular face. The deep-set brown eyes were slits against the glare as he stood above her—his legs spread apart—straddling the deck to maintain his balance. He looked to her like a tanned Adonis.

"There," he said with a smile, "we'll let Mother Nature take it from here." He dropped to his haunches and faced her. Her chin was supported by her knees. For a moment they did not speak. Mark just stared at the forest green blouse that set off her emerald eyes, and the slim blue jeans that accentuated her firm, sensual figure. He noticed her new boating shoes, and he smiled.

She caught him staring at her and noticed his smile stop at the new shoes. She patted the tops of them.

"New," she said. "I asked the salesman," she confessed, "what shoes the well-dressed sailor wears. Nothing else would do, he told me, but these." Then she looked down at the newness of them and added playfully, "I suppose I should have dirtied them up a bit, to make them look seaworthy . . ."

"Nonsense," he teased, "we'll have them soiled before the day is over. I promise you they'll be seaworthy."

"You're not going to try to turn me into whatever it is it takes to sail ol' *Flossie,* are you?" Her eyes widened in mock horror. "Believe me, I'm a novice and a dyed-in-the-wool coward when it comes to the sea. I'm content to sit here and let the captain of this ship take care of everything." She laughed. "I'm totally in your care."

He leaned his face nearer to hers, and she felt his hot breath brush her cheek. She swallowed. "But that'll never do," he said. "You'll have to

63

learn something about sailing before we return today. What if something happens to the captain. The crew has to be able to take over."

"Don't even tease like that." Tracy straightened from the waist, her shirt tightening across her chest. His eyes narrowed, following her every movement. He moistened his lips seductively.

"Okay, you're totally in my care," he said with a grin. "Now how about some coffee?" he added, still straddling his haunches.

"Great." And she watched him as he lithely unfolded himself from his squatting position. Beads of perspiration made his trim body glisten in the sun as he headed for the cabin. Tracy took a deep breath. She couldn't deny it; he definitely exuded sex.

She hugged her legs tighter and rested her head on her knees and allowed the warm sun to wash over her. He was so lean and supple, so totally at home on deck; and he had set her blood racing.

Tracy felt comfortable and secure and more wonderful than she had in a long time. It was so peaceful as the tiny waves lapped the side of the boat. How easy it must be, she thought, to be lulled to sleep aboard a boat like this. With this thought she closed her eyes and succumbed to the quiet rocking sensation of the boat.

Her sleepy green eyes opened slowly to acknowledge a large, soiled, blue deck shoe assailing her spanking new "boaters." He was quietly nudging her with his foot. Realizing where she was, she didn't lift her head but said out of the corner of her mouth, "Be careful, they set me back half a horse. I'm not too anxious to dirty 'em up just yet."

"Your coffee, m'lady." Tracy squinted against the sun as she looked up to face him. There he stood, with the sun at his back, tan and imperious, holding a mug in each hand.

"Oh, that smells sinful," she said with a wink. "Hope it's black."

"I didn't have to ask. I knew," he quipped.

She straightened abruptly to accommodate his outstretched hand and accepted the mug. With her other hand she rubbed the small of her back. Then she stood up.

"Kinky?" he asked.

She looked into his smiling eyes. "And just how do you mean that?" she asked teasingly.

"As in tight, strained, taut, uncomfortable, and so on." He sipped his coffee.

"Then I'll confess to being kinky," she replied.

The hazy sun caused Tracy to squint as she stared out at the horizon; and suddenly she was aware of the absolute stillness and quiet. She also realized how totally alone they were. She took a gulp of her coffee.

He broke the silence by asking, "Hold my cup a minute?" And as he rose, his bare leg brushed against her thigh and Tracy felt shivers shoot through her. He pulled two pillows from behind the neatly piled coiled ropes and tossed them on deck near her. "Here, we can lean back and get that sun to caress your cheeks. I believe that was one of the prerequisites for taking this trip." He crossed his ankles expertly as he lowered himself, yoga fashion, onto the red cushion.

Tracy attempted the same maneuver as a larger wave lapped the side of the boat, and she almost lost her balance. Realizing the futility of it, she just lowered herself in the normal fashion. He was certainly agile, she thought, and walked around his boat like he was on solid ground. Well, she wasn't here to compete with him, so she just sat. He was staring straight ahead with his legs crossed—one over the other—high up on each thigh. He had such strong, muscular legs; Tracy found herself fantasizing about having them wrapped around her. She swallowed more coffee.

"You okay?" he asked. "Comfortable?"

"Fine, fine," she replied. But she really wasn't; she was excited and very aware of his closeness. But she turned her head and looked at him quizzically, asking, "And, how are you? You look like an elongated pretzel."

He was sipping his coffee and snickered. "Actually, it's very relaxing; try it."

"No, thanks. I'd probably never get on a horse again."

Again he laughed and Tracy noticed how relaxed and at ease he seemed to be aboard his boat. Easy for him; meanwhile, her emotions were playing havoc with her.

He put his coffee on deck and unraveled himself. "Watch that a minute, will you, Sprite?" He walked over to adjust the sail.

She held her free hand over the mug and called, "Is that the mainsail?" She watched his hiked-up T-shirt expose his bronzed back.

He looked over his shoulder, and smiled. "Have you been fooling me? You're really a veteran sailor? And you've just been testing my abilities? For shame, Tracy Morgan," he said and turned back to his duty.

"No, no," she yelled, "I read a book once." And she watched with interest through half-slitted eyes at the tawny body pulling at the sail. The tight muscles rippled up and down his arms like massive cords. The slim hips barely supported the faded jeans, and his tan, overdeveloped legs bulged beneath his cutoffs as he bent easily with his chores. Tracy felt the beginnings of perspiration break out on her forehead. To say she was stimulated was an understatement.

In a flash he was collapsed in his comfortable position beside her and his hand fell over hers as he steadied himself. His rough, strong hand on hers for just that fleeting moment sent waves of heat through her, and she was having a hard time making small talk. "I know a few nautical words that any layman would know," she continued, and pounded the shiny deck. "I know this is the deck, that's the mainsail, and"—she threw her head back and pointed—"that's the cabin."

"You're not such a novice." He smiled.

She leaned her head back and finished her coffee. "And—you make delicious coffee."

"More?" he asked.

"If you'll join me."

"You'll never have to ask me a second time; I'm an inveterate coffee drinker. Your cup, m'lady?"

She handed it to him, and again they touched. Their eyes met and locked for one brief moment, and Tracy wondered if she weren't imagining things—or did his eyes also reflect the yearning that she felt? Her heart was pounding and her pulse rate was rapid. As he headed for the cabin, she thought, It's like electricity being unleashed when he touches me. Get hold of yourself; you've the better part of the day to handle yet.

The door to the cabin was open and she yelled to him. "Where are we headed, anyway?"

"Don't you know? I mean, can't you guess?" He smiled as he returned holding the coffee.

"I told you I'm no sailor. I only know the sun

rises in the east and sets in the west, and if I don't have the sun at my back, I never know my north from my south. And"—she took a deep breath—"what happens in between is a complete mystery to me. Why," she continued, "you could be heading us in the direction of the nearest Chinese Junk with the express purpose of selling me into white slavery."

"Tracy, Tracy, you are incorrigible. Are you always so glib?"

"Not always . . ." She paused and started to make rings with her coffee mug. Only when I'm excited and nervous, she wanted to add.

"Well," he interjected, "then I'm happy that I'm surprising you. We're heading toward Long Island; thought it'd be nice to have lunch on the North Shore."

"Lunch on Long Island? Sounds great." Tracy was so excited, she knew she'd have trouble eating —but for now—she was just going to enjoy. But, there was an ache in the pit of her stomach and she knew it had nothing to do with food.

Mark was shading his eyes with his hand as he looked to the sun that was nearly directly over them. "It's hotter than I figured it would be today." He reached into his back pocket and retrieved his sun glasses. They were the dark mirror type and Tracy could no longer see his eyes, only her own reflection in the glass.

She stood up and stretched. "Those glasses should be outlawed. I can't see your eyes; it's unfair. But"—she turned, shielding her eyes and looking at the water—"you're right; it's terribly hot. It would be great to take a swim." She placed both hands in the back pockets of her jeans and the pull made her blouse tighten at the bust. She couldn't see his eyes, but she could feel the burning stare through the glasses. She took her hands from her pockets.

Mark looked at her longingly, secure behind the dark glasses. She had such a sensual body; she was driving him wild. He was having a hard time concentrating. Maybe the water would help.

"Would you like to take a swim?" he asked huskily.

"If someone had told me to bring my suit, it would be fine."

She took a deep breath, and he tore his eyes away from her cleavage.

"We'll fix you up with something," he said, hooking his fingers in the waist of his jeans.

"Don't tell me you have several sizes of bathing suits to fit the stray females who forget . . ."

He cut her off. "My friend, Jake, has a teen-aged daughter, who's slim, just like you. Jake always leaves an old pair of cutoffs of his and his daughter's on the boat, just in case they want to change or take a quick swim." He removed his glasses and hooked them in his T-shirt. "I also have an extra T-shirt you can wear. So, are you game?" He was staring at her challengingly. He planted his legs firmly apart with his hands on his hips; he ran his tongue over his lips.

"I'm game." She stared back at him, matching his stance and tucking her shirt in her jeans. Tracy was never one to refuse a dare. She started to unbuckle her leather belt, her eyes never leaving his. He smiled a crooked smile and pulled off his T-shirt. Her eyes ran over his massive, hairy chest. She swallowed.

"I'd . . . I'd like to use that little private cabin of yours," she said in a dry voice. When he said nothing, she added in a stronger tone, "That's all right, isn't it?"

"Of course," he said in a low voice, running his fingers across his chest.

"Come on," he said, forming the words slowly, like a man coming out of a trance. "I'll—I'll get you your cutoffs and shirt." And she followed him dutifully down the few steps into the small cabin.

"Nice," she said, "very cabin-ish." He was reaching into some side drawers and finally pulled out a tiny pair of very tired, faded, old jeans. She'd barely fit into them.

"Toss your clothes on the bunk there," he said without looking at her. From another drawer he pulled out a white T-shirt with red lettering. IT'S JAKE—MAKE NO MISTAKE! was printed on the front in bold red.

"Jake's?" She held it up in front of her questioningly.

"Make no mistake!" he retorted and headed up the few steps. "He's not very original, but a very good friend. See you topside." She watched the strong legs bound toward the deck. He closed the door behind him.

Mark changed on deck and began to wonder if this whole idea of being out here alone with the woman jockey was such a good idea. He was becoming aroused, and he didn't know how much longer he could control himself. The prospect disturbed him. He was losing control and he didn't like it. She was so damned delectable: that mouth and those eyes—oh, how he could lose himself in those eyes! But the damnable part of it was that he liked her—he truly liked her; she wasn't just another female. In fact, it would be easier if she were. He didn't want to spoil anything. But he was

70

only human. He hadn't cared for anyone like this since . . . since—

"I'll be up in a minute," she called from the cabin, interrupting his thoughts. She finished tucking Jake's shirt inside her tiny cutoffs and piled her clothes neatly on the bunk. "Well, it's no designer bathing suit but it'll do." The cabin was hot and she welcomed the breeze as she reached the deck.

His back was to her as she came up behind him and Tracy noticed the strong muscles of his tanned back. She had an uncontrollable urge to reach out and grab him around the waist. Instead, she called out, "First mate reporting, sir."

He turned and paused, his slitted eyes devouring her. He swallowed audibly. "I—I've dropped anchor, so we won't drift. Well, let's go," and he dove overboard. So much for gallantry, Tracy thought.

She dove in after him and found the water was delightful and refreshing. When she peeked above the surface, pushing her long hair back from her face, he was only inches away, splashing around noisily.

"Cooled off?" he asked, and without waiting for a reply, he began to swim away from the boat. His hair was plastered flat round his head and the droplets running down his sun-tanned face and neck made him look like a Greek god. Tracy gulped a deep swallow of air.

"Yes, it's great, but I'm afraid I'd have trouble keeping up with you—in the water."

"I'm glad you clarified." He smiled. "Let's swim around the boat a few times and work up an appetite." He was a powerful swimmer, and Tracy had all she could do to keep pace with him, but she did.

They circled the boat twice, and Tracy was

71

happy when he suggested they go on board. One more minute and she would have had to give up.

He helped her aboard, dripping over her as she reached up for his strong arm. He grabbed a towel and tossed her one; she wrapped her long auburn hair in it, making a turban of it.

When Mark had finished rubbing off his chest and looked up, his mouth opened. He gasped. The water was running off her slim body and making a puddle on the deck. She stood there like a statuesque madonna. His blood raced. His unabashed stare traveled from her long, slim, muscular legs to the soaking wet, tight cut-off jeans, to the dripping wet, nearly transparent "Jake's" T-shirt. It clung to her chest, allowing her full, firm breasts to stand out shamelessly against the thin white material.

He threw his towel over his shoulders and stared at her.

"You'd better go below and change—quickly— before something happens."

Tracy stood there like a block of granite, dripping wet, saying nothing. He inched toward her. "I'm warning you, Tracy; you're not toying with one of your boy jockeys." He took a few more steps and stood so close to her that she could feel his hot breath on her face. "I'm warning you," he repeated in a low, controlled tone. "Say something, damn it." His voice was husky with emotion.

Her lips parted, and in a low, sultry voice she said, "You don't have to threaten me." Her wet tongue darted out, moistening her sensual mouth.

He could feel himself coloring; a surge welled within him so strong that he was in danger of losing all control. She stood fast. "Okay," he said. He was like a bull in heat. He leaned over to meet the wet tongue. His mouth was pressing, demanding, and he was panting. His wet chest was crushing hers. His anxious fingers ran over her soaking T-shirt, fondling her full breasts. Her nipples became hard and her chest was heaving. She clawed at his back and he bit into her neck. His hand cupped her breast and massaged her nipple. He called her name and buried his tongue in her open, waiting mouth—surging, exploring. Her head dropped back and she moaned.

He picked her up as if she were weightless and squeezed her body closer to his and headed for the cabin and kicked the door open. He pulled off her turban and tossed her on the bunk. Her wet hair spread across the covers invitingly. Leaning over her, he threw her neatly folded clothes on the cabin floor and climbed on the bunk with her. Straddling her body, his strong legs pinned her to the bed. Her green eyes were beguiling half slits, shaded by long black lashes. He stared at her, then inched forward, his arms supporting him while he looked down at the creamy, white skin flushed with excitement.

"Tracy," he cried with passion, and his lips went down to lay claim to her waiting mouth. He relaxed his arms and slid beside her, never breaking the kiss. She moaned and he crushed her body close to him. His hand reached to the button and zipper of the clinging, wet jeans, and he slowly pulled the zipper down. His hand patiently crawled upward beneath the wet T-shirt, ever so slowly. He didn't want to rush; he wanted the moment to last, but he couldn't wait to take her—to have her fully.

The tips of his fingers found the nipples of her breasts and caressed them into hard rocks. He was at her throat, tormenting her with his tongue. The experienced hand slowly slid from the breasts to the firm, flat stomach. Tracy ached with passion and thought if their bodies didn't meet fully soon, she'd explode. He leaned over her again, and pulled off the T-shirt.

"Oh, my God," he exclaimed, and he lowered his head to her chest. His mouth and tongue played with the hard tips of her breasts, making her writhe with pleasure.

She began to claw at him and scream and his mouth went to hers, silencing the groans—first tenderly, then passionately, and then more demandingly. Her lips parted eagerly, her hot breath coming in short gasps, and then she, too, was hungrily searching his mouth with her tongue—exploring, feeling, surveying.

Tracy's blood was surging; her head was reeling. With one strong hand, he held her steady; the other slipped between her legs. She moaned and her fingers tangled in his hair. She was caught up in a force, a maelstrom of emotion, which sent her senses spiraling into the outer cosmos. Tracy was in an unexplored area. Low sounds of contentment escaped her raw lips.

He raised his head and looked at her, and his fingers ran up and down Tracy's slim body. He began to tug the shorts from her slim hips. He maneuvered them down her legs, and she willingly lifted her feet to accommodate him. He tossed the shorts to the floor and stared at her beautiful nakedness. She reached up to unfasten his shorts, but he eased himself from the bunk, pulled off his jeans, and returned to her, once again straddling her firm body. He caressed her, playing her body like a fine-tuned instrument—tormenting her—driving her to another plateau of desire. His tongue started a passage from her neck down to her breasts and to her stomach and upper thighs. She screamed out finally, unable to hold it in any longer. "Mark! Stop teasing me—Mark, please . . ."

Then he lowered himself onto her. She knew there could never be another time like this. Ever! He held her closer and closer, and tiny gasps escaped her. She was falling into an abyss and there was no escape—no return—and she didn't want to return. She wanted to stay here forever. His mouth sought hers again, and she returned the brutal kiss eagerly, matching him in his ferocity and heat. She squirmed and screamed and demanded more, and he gave her everything she screamed for and still she wasn't sated.

Then suddenly a flood opened within her and she screamed his name over and over again.

Now it was he who spoke huskily, "You're like a she-devil, uncontrollable and wild." And Mark Flanagan knew he had found his match in this challenging female. She moaned and called him again, and he came to her; the heat emanating from his lean, firm body, the perspiration flooding between them, and they swayed together and called each other by name until exhaustion overtook them, and he slipped from her hot satiated body onto the bunk beside her.

He gasped, allowing a long sigh to fill the cabin. A tiny smile curled the end of his mouth, and he thought, Here I am, the man who didn't want a serious commitment, who ran constantly, trying to escape. And now I return home and discover in my own backyard, a filly as feisty and demanding as I am myself. No holds barred. You bet your *Flossie*, you're committed, he told himself.

75

"Tracy . . ."

"Mark," she turned her face toward him and kissed him lightly on the mouth. There were tiny wet ringlets surrounding her high forehead. "Please, don't say anything." She was frightened of what he might tell her, afraid of being turned down, of finding out he didn't care for her as much as she knew she cared for him. She couldn't take that. So, she'd rather not have her dreams dashed. Tracy was so in love, she'd take him any way that she could, and if it meant just being added to the already large number of lovers, well, she'd settle for that—for now. She wanted no false hopes—no promises. Deep down, however, she knew there was something between them, and she was going to make certain it remained.

"Mark, don't say anything, not just yet. Let's just see what turns out . . ."

He leaned over on one elbow. "What are you talking about?" And he took her head and nuzzled it cozily in the crook of his neck. "You're like a breath of fresh air to me, warm and sunny and bright . . ."

"This isn't going to be a weather report, is it?" she quipped.

"Tracy, Tracy," he said and laughed, rumpling her already tangled hair. "I'm crazy about you— what's the matter with you? Can't you see that?" He plopped her head back on the bunk unceremoniously, and again supported himself with his elbow. He looked into the flushed, open face. "What do you think that was all about? Don't you know when someone cares about you?"

"Well, yes, but . . ." She was thrilled. He did care. He did! He did!

"But, nothing—" he countered. "I don't under-

76

stand you. Don't you want to make an honest man of me?" And he leaned over and kissed her swollen lips. "You are a hellcat, and I love it." He kissed her eyes.

"I just didn't want to make any demands . . ."

"Hush, Sprite; I'll let you know when you're demanding, and," he added huskily, "if that's any indication of your demands, I'll take them any time."

She blushed right through the already red-raw skin. She was tingling with happiness . . .

"Look," he glanced down, all wisdom, Tracy thought, "there's something here between us, right?" She happily nodded her assent. "Well, let's just give it a chance." He kissed her before she could object. Then he drew back and looked at her glowing face. "Those eyes will drive me crazy yet." He inched over her slim frame and bounded from the bunk. He looked down at her and smiled, dropping his fingers to caress her outstretched arm. She looked up and saw where the bronze ended at the neck of his T-shirt and at the uneven line from his cutoffs. He leaned over her and whispered, "I don't know about you, lady, but this guy could use another dip in that water. What do you say? And," he winked, "I don't think you'll feel too self-conscious to go without your shorts and T-shirt this time."

She reached both arms up and caught him around the neck. "No, for some strange reason, I won't."

He laughed, kissed her, reached into the cabinet, and grabbed two fresh towels and ran out on deck. She obediently ran after him, and they both dove into the water. He stretched his arms toward her and she eased herself into his cool embrace.

She wrapped her legs around his waist and leaned back splashing her arms about her. The water was like a blanket, and she felt cool and wonderful as she clung to him.

A cool breeze was beginning to cause tiny ripples to dance across the blue water. They swam several times around the boat and then his hand guided her toward the rope dangling over the boat's side. He was aboard in one leap, and he helped her up and tossed a towel in her direction.

"Wonderful—it felt wonderful." She rubbed her face roughly with the towel and then wrapped it around her, securing it in front.

Tracy pushed her long hair back from her face and experienced chills as the afternoon's breeze danced over her wet body. Mark turned to her, his towel tied around his waist. She stared at the massive tanned chest and the wet curly hair that adorned it.

He stared back at her, looking at the trim body wrapped in the white towel. The sun was caressing her body and the breeze whipped a corner of the towel free, exposing a muscular thigh. In two strides he was in front of her. "We'd better go below. There's a breeze whipping up, Tracy; I don't want you to catch cold."

"I don't think I could," she said throatily, looking up into the tanned face.

Without another word he picked her up again and headed toward the cabin. This time he placed her tenderly into the bunk and slowly opened the towel and caressed her breasts. She shuddered.

"Mark . . ." escaped from her lips, but that's all he allowed her. He leaned over and kissed her lightly, sensually, then more passionately. His tongue sought release in the wet hollow of her mouth. His hand traveled up and down her body lightly, just the fingertips caressing, teasing. She moaned.

"Not yet," he said huskily, "not yet, my spitfire." Tracy was like a tightly coiled spring. Her muscles tightened and released as his thumb brushed her nipples. She groaned, and his hand went down over the tight stomach and reached between her thighs. She nearly screamed.

"Mark, Mark—please . . ." Both her hands shot up and clasped him behind his neck urging him down, down, closer to her. He opened the towel at his waist and rolled, gently, on top of her, supporting himself with his elbows. She dug her nails into his neck. "Please—please," she pleaded.

His mouth was buried in the nape of her neck, and he could feel the fire of her skin. He could stand no more. "Now," the words escaped brusquely, "now, my little hellcat." His mouth sought hers fiercely, and a crescendo crashed within Tracy's hot brain. She was hurtled head-long into an interminable black vacuum, and she didn't care; she didn't want to return.

They matched each other's passion—enjoying, experiencing, exploring—and when Tracy thought she could take no more, he would pull back from her and make her demand more.

Finally, their hot passion expended, it was replaced by tender, rapturous embraces. Exhausted, they both sighed happily, spent in their passion. They lay side by side, silently, and Tracy turned languorously in his muscular arms. He placed her hand on his chest, and she could feel through the hot, sweaty body the fierce, rhythmic pumping of his heart.

He reached down and pulled up a thin sheet

blanket rolled at the bottom of the bunk, and covered them.

"Now, I feel secure," she said, nuzzling into his chest. He cupped her chin in his hand and raised her face toward his. Her skin was aglow and Mark thought he had never seen anyone so lovely. He reached over and touched her face tenderly. She took his hand in hers and kissed the palm with her tongue.

He pulled his hand away quickly. "Please, Trace, it takes very little to get me aroused; you'll kill me!"

"Wouldn't do that. You know I'm no sailor; I'd be stranded."

He kissed her nose. "Tease," he said and hiked himself up and looked out the tiny porthole. "Umm, still warm. Would you like a cold drink?"

"I don't know. Is it time? I mean, is the sun over the yardarm yet, or whatever it is that you sailors demand of that first drink?" She pulled her legs up under the sheet to meet her chest, so he could slip by her.

"They only say that in old British B movies." He laughed as he inched out of the bunk. "Besides, I was thinking of a Coke," and he wrapped his towel around him.

"In the interest of modesty?" she asked, turning on her side facing his backside and his strong, long legs as he bent down and retrieved two Cokes from a mini-refrigerator.

"No," he said and snickered, handing her the Coke and sitting on the edge of the bunk beside her warm body. "In the interest of self-preservation."

They both laughed and Tracy colored slightly.

They sipped their drinks, their eyes meeting and smiling.

Mark pushed his head back and drained the remainder of his drink. He looked toward the porthole. "I must apologize . . ."

"For what?" She pulled the sheet up to her neck, eyes wide.

"For not making it over to the other side for lunch. Do you realize," he looked at her, "we haven't eaten all day? And, if I'm to keep up my strength . . ." He reached beneath the sheet and patted her warm thigh playfully.

"Oh." She blushed, knowing how the sentence was to end. "Your hands are cold," she said and shook her leg free of him. He removed his hand.

"Anyway, it's too late for lunch, hussy." He winked. "So, since Long Island is ruled out, I'll take you to an early dinner in Connecticut. There's a very unsophisticated fish and chips place, where one does *not* have to dress for dinner."

"Does that mean I have to wear Jake's T-shirt?" Her tongue licked the top of the Coke can.

"No, my love, you can wear your own clothes. And, I'm sure I have another pair of jeans around here. All I meant was it's not fancy or pretentious, but the food is tremendous. Do you mind?"

"You're the skipper," she returned. "Of course, I don't mind; I love being relaxed and not having to dress up."

"You do?" he said surprised. "That's great—me, too." And he leaned over and kissed her sweet, wet mouth. "I guess we've got a lot to discover about each other, Miss Tracy . . ."

"I guess we do, Mr. Mark." She propped her

81

head on her knees and lowered her eyes. "Great, isn't it?" And she meant it.

"Umm," he said, tasting her sweet soda lips. "Great, but God, I'm ravenous; you must be starving, too, Trace. We haven't eaten all day."

"I guess I am a little hungry," she said and leaned back on her elbows. "Now if you'll just let me get dressed." She pointed to her clothes tossed in a heap where he had thrown them in the heat of passion. And both remembered the moment that seemed eons ago, and Mark colored as he silently picked them up and handed them to her.

"Well, hurry up." He straightened, tightening the towel around his waist. "I want to show you the beautiful sunset."

"Already?" She raised an eyebrow and craned her neck in an attempt to see past him.

"It must be sunset by now. You've kept me quite busy all day . . ." He winked and ran from the cabin onto the deck where a cool breeze was blowing.

"Why, you egotistical . . ." The cabin door slammed behind him.

Tracy eased herself into the tiny lavatory and washed her face. She looked into the mirror. My God, I look as if I've been ravished. You have, Tracy, ol' girl, you have, a tiny voice told her. She smiled contentedly back at her reflection. She washed herself as best she could in the confining quarters and brushed her hair. Her stomach was growling and she looked down and said, "Be still, you'll be fed soon." And for the first time in days, she wasn't concerned with her weight. Tracy Morgan was happy—ecstatic. She was in love.

He was bent over coiling a line as Tracy emerged on deck, the muscles tightening down his back as he made the continuous motion, piling one neat circle atop the other. He was wearing a new pair of jeans and a clean, light blue shirt. The bright rays of the sun played across the strong back and caused yellow streaks to highlight his dark hair. Tracy had an uncontrollable urge to walk up behind him and slip her arms around him. Instead, she called casually, "Need a hand?"

"Nope," he replied, without breaking momentum, "I could do this in my sleep."

He dropped the last piece down inside the coil and straightened, rubbing his back.

"Kinky?" she asked.

"Very." He laughed as he turned to her. The same rainbow of colors was dancing across Tracy's body, and he paused for a moment and said nothing. Then he walked toward her and took her hand. "We'll be coming in soon; come, stand by the rail with me and watch the sunset." He took her aft and they stood together as a cool breeze touched them. Short, choppy waves were forming as they watched the huge fire ball that had started their day, slowly begin its descent. Fiery red, purple, and gold streamed across the horizon like disparate colored ribbons.

"It's breathtaking," she whispered. "I've never seen anything so beautiful. No wonder you love it so."

"It's a sight you never tire of, Tracy."

"I can see why. It's almost like—like . . ." She paused. "Like bringing home a winner!"

He laughed and squeezed her hand. "That's quite an analogy. You are your father's daughter— a true thoroughbred. C'mon, we're almost in." He grabbed an oar laying on the side of the deck. "Here, you wanted to do something . . ."

"We're rowing in?"

"No, feisty, I just use it to keep the boat from hitting the dock as we pull in." He handed her the oar and added, "Then, I'll tie her off . . ."

"I knew you'd have me doing something nautical before we got back."

"Okay, that's good; now just steady her." He jumped over the rail and landed noiselessly on the dock, secured the boat, and came back to offer her his hand.

He lifted her over the railing in one swoop. They stood close together as the last of the sun's rays burnished the warped, wooden dock.

"Come, Tracy, my love," he said, slipping his hand around her waist. "Time to eat."

"Right. I'm hungry." She smiled up at him.

"Well, good; that's the first time I've heard that from you." He took her by the hand and headed her toward the car. "Josie's Bar awaits us—cuisine supreme!"

Tracy looked back at the water as she climbed into the car. A perfect day, from sunup to sundown. She wished she could make time stop to frame this moment. He slammed his door, dissolving her mood, and started the engine.

As they drove, she sat close to him, and the warmth of his leg next to hers was a pleasant experience. They climbed a slight hill, made several turns, and came down another hill to face the water again and a little ramshackle building that had to have been a barn at one time but was now turned into a restaurant. A sign flashed on and off proclaiming it to be Josie's.

"Rustic enough?" he asked as he turned off the car.

"Downright remote," she conceded. "I never even knew this existed."

"Come," he said, "we can still get a table by the window and watch day turn into night."

And they did just that. As they sipped drinks, the first gray of night was pushing all the pink from the sky, casting the remainder of the rainbow colors further to the west. They toasted each other, enjoying the final light of the day, anticipating the first shadows of evening.

The fish arrived—fried—and Tracy cringed. Mark caught the look of dissatisfaction on her face and asked, "Anything wrong, Trace?" He gave her an engaging smile.

"No, no—just that it's fried." She toyed with the fish.

"That's the only way fish and chips come, Sprite. This is what they're noted for here. We *did* agree on this, didn't we?" He put his knife and fork down. "Do you want me to order you something *broiled?*" He made the word sound dirty, and there was a decided edge of annoyance to his voice.

Tracy stiffened at his tone, but said quietly, in the best controlled voice she could muster, "No, no, this'll be fine." And she took a bountiful bite of her fried flounder. "Umm, good; you're right—nothing like fried!" She could feel her hips spreading.

He resumed eating and Tracy followed suit. Finally, she sighed and put her fork down. "That was great."

He looked up. "That's it? You've only finished half."

"Oh, believe me, that's plenty; I have to maintain my fighting weight, you know." She cupped her chin in her hands and smiled at him coquettishly. She thought, For this little repast, I'm going to have to starve for days! But she didn't want to spoil the day. It had been so perfect. Then she bent over and asked conspiratorially, "I could use some coffee, though."

He ordered the coffee and pushed his unfinished plate aside.

"You're not finishing?" After she had said it, she wanted to bite her tongue.

The dark eyes looked up at her. "I'm full, too. Besides, as I've mentioned before, I do not enjoy eating alone . . ."

"That's not fair, Mark, I'm here . . ." The waitress brought the coffee and Tracy fell silent. After she left, Mark slipped his hand over Tracy's and she looked up at him. She could see, however, that he was still annoyed.

He took a sip of coffee and looked at her. "I just don't want to see you ruining . . ."

Tracy leaned across the table and put her index finger to his lips. "Did anyone ever tell you that you're *beautiful* when you're angry?" She was determined not to have the day spoiled.

He threw his head back and laughed good-naturedly. "Okay, okay, I relent." And he turned his palms up yielding to her.

The tenseness gone, they chatted amiably and finished their coffee. Mark paid the bill and Tracy walked outside. He ushered her into the car. As they drove, a light drizzle started and the rhythmic sound of the windshield wipers began to mesmerize Tracy. She felt her eyes closing, and she didn't fight it. She put her head on his shoulder and Mark smiled down at her.

He pulled in front of her house and Tracy's eyes

flew open when he turned the engine off. "Oh, I must have dozed off . . ."

"Did anyone ever tell you that you snore?"

"Oh, no—I didn't?" she sat upright, questioning.

"No, but you must have been exhausted. I think," he paused, "you need more nutrition."

"We're not going to start on *that* again, are we?" She stiffened. "You have to realize I have my career at stake; it's important to me."

"More important than your health?" he interjected.

"I am perfectly healthy, I assure you."

"Okay, okay; I can see I've hit on your Achilles' heel. Let's forget it." There was a coolness to his voice that she did not like.

"Yes, let's," she replied. She looked straight ahead and cleared her throat. When he said nothing, her hand moved to the car door handle. "Well, I have to be up early, and . . ."

"Me, too," he finished.

She reached for the handle, stopped, and they both started to speak at once. "Mark . . ."

"Tracy . . ."

They were in each other's arms in an instant. He hugged her and pulled her very close to him, and Tracy felt that she belonged there. He was whispering in her ear, "Don't say anything, please." Slowly, he pushed her away, looking into the pale face. "I'll call you."

He released her and Tracy slowly slid across the car seat and pushed the door open. She stepped outside the car and slammed the door. She was looking straight ahead as he started the engine and maneuvered the car down the driveway. Again, she felt chastised. "I'll call you"—well, isn't that nice," she stormed out loud. "Dropped like a cheap suit!" She kicked at the pebbles with her new boaters.

While they hadn't exactly quarreled, their parting was less than what she had expected. Damn him and his nutrition!

But, thinking of the day's events, she smiled and turned her face toward the light drizzle and let it caress her face. Today had been wonderful.

Tracy was about to run up the front steps when she could see the outline of her father and Gus in the den. She quickly darted around to the back of the house and raced up the back stairs into her room. She threw herself across the bed.

Tiny tears, unsolicited, assailed her cheeks, and she was torn between an ecstatic happiness and a nagging concern as she patted her stomach. She leaned her arm over her eyes and brushed the tears with her shirt-sleeve. The arm remained there, blocking out the light from the front yard that peeked from between her curtains. In the darkness a scene materialized: tiny whitecaps danced across a sunny Long Island Sound, and strong arms were holding her in a passionate embrace. Cutting through the happy scene were stern words, "You need more nutrition . . ."

Tracy tore off her clothes and crawled beneath the covers. She had an early call; she had to work out two new fillies in the morning. But through the night a familiar face would float above her with chastising deep-set brown eyes.

"Mark, Mark," she cried, and she remembered the burning passion of his kiss and the strong hands that played over her body. "Just love me, that's all I ask."

"Well, don't snap my head off," Scotty bellowed. "I only asked you where you were last night. I called to tell you that Brady's stable called me and asked if you could work out one of his horses while you were here this morning. I said you wouldn't mind, and I thought you might want to get here earlier—"

She cut him off. "Isn't six o'clock early enough?" she asked sharply, offering him her backside as she bent over, adjusting her pants inside her boots.

"My, my, aren't we a wee bit touchy today? You never complained before about coming out early. But you do need your rest, you know, if you're going to do your best. After all . . ."

"Et tu Brute," she mumbled under her breath. She lowered her leg from the bench, straightened up, and tucked her blouse inside her jeans and faced him. Tracy felt as if she were being reprimanded by too many males. "Back up a little, Scotty, I'm not accountable to you as to my whereabouts—*all* of the time." She grabbed her jacket and headed toward the track where Harry was waiting for her to mount.

"Hey, Trace." He quickly caught up with her. "I just meant that I thought you'd be pleased. You're making a name for yourself and people are asking about you."

She took a deep breath and let the cool air attack her lungs. "I do love the early morning," she said; then, turning to Scotty, she playfully tapped him on his shoulder with her riding crop. "Sorry, if I was a little late; didn't sleep that well, Buddha." She gave him an engaging smile. "I'll be glad to work out Brady's horse."

"That's my lass." He smiled, exposing tobacco-stained teeth.

Tracy reached Harry, who was singing and patting the horse as he straightened her reins.

"Hi, Tracy," he yelled. "Runnin' a bit late, aren't we?" Tracy decided that they were definitely in consort against her; there was a conspiracy afoot.

"That's me, ol' Tardy Tracy," she quipped. "Instead of keeping a time check, would you mind giving me a leg up?"

"My pleasure, Tracy." The groom bent over and cupped his hands. She pushed her boot into his strong hands and the other leg flew over the chestnut filly in a flash.

"Okay. Let's go, girl." She drew back on the reins and was off, taking the horse through her paces and breaking into an easy canter as they breezed around the track.

Harry and Scotty leaned over the railing and watched her. Her body was one with the horse, and they seemed to glide effortlessly through the early morning's mist.

"That lady can ride," Harry said with a smile, his huge white teeth brightening his face.

"She sure can, lad, she sure can." Scotty rubbed the stubble on his chin and lit another cigarette.

Tracy raced several mounts that morning and finally Scotty called for her to take a rest. She pulled up and patted Brady's horse and said, "She's a good little filly." She slid from the horse expertly, and patted it tenderly. "Good girl."

"C'mon, Tracy, you've got to have a little rest . . ."

"Okay, Scotty, okay; guess I could use a break." She handed the reins to Harry and walked toward the stalls with Scotty. Her face was flushed, and she removed her hat to let her hair spill down and wiped her brow with her jacket sleeve. The sun had burned off the morning's mist and it was beginning to warm up. Tiny sparrows were picking at bits of food on the grounds, and as they approached, the birds flew toward the trees in a loud rush. Tracy was following their flight, and not watching where she was walking, when she stepped on a rock and turned her ankle.

"Oh, no . . ."

Scotty grabbed her to avoid her falling.

"Are you all right, lass?" He was leading her to a bench by the stalls.

"I—I think so." But it hurt. She sat down and rubbed her ankle.

"Here," Scotty was saying, concerned, "let's take off that boot and have a look . . ."

"Oh, Scot, don't be an old lady. It'll be all right. I'll just . . ."

"You'll just listen to me," he said authoritatively. "I am your trainer and I do know about sprained ankles . . ." He pulled the boot off carefully.

"Don't say that," she implored. But Tracy winced when he removed the boot.

She pulled off her sock and his trained hands turned the ankle this way and that. "Hmm," he said, surveying it. "It's starting to swell already. I'm going to call Doc Olsen; he's over by the paddock. Now don't put any weight on it and keep it raised on the bench like this." He pulled it gently to one side, the bench supporting her entire leg.

"No, no," Tracy called as he walked away, "I'll be okay . . ." But as her voice trailed off, even she knew it wasn't going to be okay. It hurt and she watched the right slim ankle turn into a fat blob.

Doc Olsen was short and squat, spent most of his income on "worthy nags," and was not given to lengthy medical explanations.

"Hmm, hmm—yep."

"Could you translate that medical opinion into layman—in this case, laywoman's—terms, Doc?"

He looked up from beneath bushy white eyebrows as his soft white hands held her swollen foot. "Sprained, Tracy, m'dear. Too bad, too. I was going to bet you in tomorrow's race. Shame, too; you were doin' great."

"What? You mean I can't ride tomorrow?" she asked, as if the prospect was implausible. She raised an arched eyebrow. "But, I must . . ."

"Not tomorrow—or for several more days. Look at that ankle, miss," and he pointed now to an angry red swelling. "You won't get a boot on that foot for six—maybe seven days. You're to go home, keep it up with your weight off it, and take it easy. I'll stop by to see you in a few days."

"Oh, no," she cried.

"Oh, yes," he countered, "and you'd better do as you're told—or it'll wind up being longer." He straightened to his full five foot five and pulled at a flabby jowl. "Shame, too, The Cricket looked like a good entry in tomorrow's third race."

Tracy was livid. Here she was, going to be laid up for several days with a painful ankle, and all he could think of was his bet in tomorrow's race.

"You'll just have to live with it, Doc," she said caustically. "But cheer up, someone else'll ride it."

"Now, now, Tracy, don't be flippant. I only meant, I would have preferred to have seen you ride it."

"Me, too, Doc," she returned with a sarcastic grin. "Me, too."

"All right, Tracy, all right. It's not the end of the world. Just a few days. It'll give you a chance to rest up and relax." Then he turned to Scotty and

Harry. "Make sure you get her right home and tell Bull what I've told you."

"Right, Doc, right you are," Scotty said, twisting his cap in his hands. "I knew it, I knew it."

Then, turning to Tracy, and holding his black bag tightly with his two pudgy hands across his fat thighs, the doctor asked, "You got an old pair of crutches around?"

"A set in each room, Doc."

He laughed, the blood racing to his face, and he looked to Tracy like a cuddly little cherub. "You're Bull Morgan's daughter all right."

Scotty interrupted. "I have an old pair, Doc; I'll bring 'em over."

"See that you do. She'll need 'em when she hops to the john." Then, turning back to Tracy, he patted her knee. "Take care." He walked away, shaking his head. "What a shame—she could've brought that nag in . . ."

Tracy was touched by his solicitude. She pointed to her foot and motioned to Scotty and Harry. "You'll have to help me to my feet—correction—my foot." She smiled wanly.

Scotty tossed Harry his keys. "Bring the car to the front gate; I'll carry her there as soon as you're parked."

"Right." Harry tapped his fingers to his cap in a mock salute. "I'll only be a minute." He raced off.

"Oh, damn." Tracy sighed. "Just when everything was beginning to come together."

"It'll be fine, lass. A few days rest and relaxation . . ."

"You sound like Doc Olsen. Are you two rehearsing the same scenario?" She leaned on one elbow looking down at her ankle.

"Oh, buck up, lass."

93

"Your next line isn't going to be, 'You'll see, when you're better, we'll give 'em hell, kid,' is it? I don't think I can take any more of this pep talk. And, what is all this rest and relaxation nonsense? You know I can't be idle; I have to be active."

"Now, now, lass, settle down." Harry just then tooted the car horn and Scotty scooped her up like she was a bag of popcorn.

"Can you handle it?" She smiled, resigned to her days of r and r.

"You and three like ya." He winked. "Why, lass, you're as light as—as . . ."

"As Bull Morgan's empty boot?" she whispered.

"Ssh, lass," he said and laughed. "That's a family secret." And he carried her to the car.

Tracy laid her head on Scotty's shoulder and allowed him to herd her into his beatup Buick. She wished, however, that it was someone else's strong arms that were lifting her—and carrying her toward that wonderful, lumpy, uncomfortable bunk bed.

CHAPTER FIVE

Mark didn't call the first day or the second, and all Tracy's rest and relaxation was turning into nervous tension. Normally, she would turn down the food that her father brought her, but she was so anxious that she picked without realizing what she was doing. She read till her eyes ached, watched outside her window as the grooms worked the horses, and stared at the phone that didn't ring for her.

Tracy was lonesome. She missed her horses, and she desperately missed the tall, rugged lover of her dreams. Why didn't he call? Could those few words of the other night have set him into a temper? Maybe something happened to him. But she knew that couldn't be; she would have heard. There were no secrets around the track. Thinking of the track, she laughed. Old Doc Olsen must be cursing her, she thought. The Cricket did run the other day but came in sixth. She knew that if she had been riding him, she would have brought him in.

Tracy raised herself up on her elbows from the chaise lounge that had been arranged for her by the window and looked down at the ankle that was the cause of her forced retirement. Not too bad, she conceded. The swelling was disappearing.

Maybe she could start moving around earlier than Doc had anticipated.

Tracy leaned back and sighed. This was the end of the fourth day and she was developing cabin fever. The phone rang and she jumped from her seat. Sally, the massive housekeeper and cook, answered it. She hated the phone; it took her from her kitchen. Anything that disturbed her from her sunny, well-equipped sanctuary was an intrusion, and the party on the other end usually incurred her wrath.

"All right, then, I'll tell her," she answered in her clipped tone and dropped the receiver into the cradle. Sally had all the subtlety of a drunken panhandler.

"That was the Doc," she yelled, heading back to her retreat. "He'll be here in the mornin' to look at your foot."

"Thanks, Sal," Tracy returned. Maybe, she thought, the Doc'll tell me I can get up earlier. After all, her ankle was looking very good, and she lifted it, turning it every way possible to make it appear slimmer.

"Beautiful," a sharp voice came from behind her. Tracy's foot plopped back to the feathery pillow. Sally stood in the doorway with her hands on her hips, her feet spread apart. She held a huge wooden mixing spoon in her left fist, and to Tracy it looked almost like a lethal weapon. "Tea?"

"Oh, I didn't hear you, Sal."

"Well, do you want tea or not? I'm brewing a pot." She wiped the few gray stray strands of hair that drooped into her eyes with the back of her hand.

Oh, no, Tracy thought, not that dark tea that you could skate on. But she didn't want to offend Sally.

"Maybe you could just make me one of those herb teas that you have in the kitchen? Don't feel like caffeine today."

"You mean, that *you* have," she corrected. "Such nonsense; what you need is a good strong cup of tea, steeped till it's black." She didn't budge an inch and filled the doorway like an ominous tank.

"Just an herb tea, please, Sally." Tracy smiled her most beguiling smile.

Sally was a huge woman with very set ideas. "Don't understand how you can drink that stuff." She shook her massive head back and forth as she turned her back on Tracy and headed for the kitchen, mumbling, "looks like somethin' you'd put in a birdbath." She nearly made it to her retreat when the phone rang again. A resounding grunt filled the hallway. "Who? Tracy?" she said. "Of course she's here—can't go very far with a twisted ankle. Hold on," the command came, and she dropped the phone on the little oak table.

Ah, Sally, you've missed your calling, Tracy said silently. You should have entered the diplomatic corp. "Who is it?" Tracy asked out loud, watching the huge form bend over and put the spare phone in the jack near Tracy's chaise lounge. She was puffing when she handed Tracy the phone.

"Didn't ask." She straightened, red-faced. "But it sounds like one of those little guys. . . ."

"Oh," Tracy said and sighed disappointedly. "Little guys" was the term Sally used for jockeys, and no amount of coaching or prodding could induce her to use another term.

"Hello?" Tracy said woefully.

"Tracy? Tracy? Is that you?" Recognizing the voice, Tracy bolted upright.

"Mark?" Her eyes widened and flew to the massive creature who was standing over her like a sentinel with her hands glued to her huge hips. Tracy put her hand over the phone and whispered to Sally, "It's for me . . ." She jerked her head in the direction of the kitchen with eyes that pleaded that she leave the room.

"Hmmph, I know it's for you!" she said, storming out, "and from the looks of ya, it's not one of the little guys . . ."

"Tracy? What's going on? Who was that?"

"Just Sally—cook, housekeeper, overseer," she said cheerfully. She was thrilled to hear his voice and held the phone with both hands as if to bring him nearer to her.

"What have you done to yourself? I called yesterday, but he said you were resting; so, I said not to disturb you . . ."

"Who said?" she interrupted.

"Why, Scotty, your trainer. All I could get out of him was that you were laid up, and I told him I'd call back."

Why, that devil, she thought. He never mentioned anything to her. But it didn't matter. She was ecstatic; he had called.

"Mark, where are you? You sound so far away."

"Up in Boston . . ."

"Boston? But why . . . ?"

"Never mind that now, Trace. What have you done to yourself? I can't leave you for a minute. Was it your leg—or your foot?"

"My ankle," she corrected, "and it wasn't intentional, believe me. I wasn't looking where I was walking and a rock that had it in for me somehow got under my foot. Anyway, I sprained my ankle and I'm spending all my time with my feet in the air. I should be fine in a few days."

There was a slow release of air from the other end. "Good—at least it's nothing more serious than your ankle. I was—I was—"

Say it, damn you, I'm not going to help you. "Yes?" she whispered huskily into the phone.

"Well, I was concerned . . ."

God forbid you should say "worried"—but, I guess "concerned" comes a close second, she thought. Tracy settled for "concerned."

"So was I," she replied. "In this business the legs are important." She paused. "But, I'm obeying orders and the doctor will be here tomorrow, so I'm hoping I'll be up and in the saddle soon."

"Don't rush it, Tracy, please; if you walk on it too soon, you'll only incur a setback and . . ."

"Incur a setback!" Why did she sometimes feel that he was speaking to her from a podium? She smiled into the phone. "I won't, *Doctor* Flanagan. But, enough of me. Tell me, please, what are you doing in Boston?"

"Well, it was business—some real estate deals I'm working on. But, believe me, if I had known that you had hurt yourself, I would have canceled the trip. Anyway, I'll tell you all about it when I see you. Now," he continued in a more concerned tone of voice, "are you sure you're taking care of yourself?" He didn't wait for her to answer but rambled on, "I wish I could catch a flight tonight— to be near you. I should be with you."

Tracy leaned back and cradled the phone, a tiny smile creasing the corners of her mouth. It was so wonderful to hear from him and know he was worried and upset. He didn't always say the exact words she wanted to hear, but it was great just to

99

listen to his dialogue. She could picture his fingers running through his thick, dark hair, and the nervous smile that crept through the handsome, tanned face, and she snuggled deeper and more contentedly into her chaise.

He was still talking. ". . . I'm just sorry I wasn't there, but I should be able to make it back tomorrow."

"That's wonderful," Tracy said in her most seductive voice.

"Yes, yes, it is," he stuttered. He cleared his throat. "Tracy, I . . ."

"Yes, Mark?"

"Tracy, I miss you . . ."

"Do you? Do you really?" She answered anxiously, moving forward in the lounge, sophistication and mystery flying out the window. "I miss you, too, Mark . . ."

"Trace, I'll be in on a six o'clock flight. I'll rush from the airport, all right? I mean, you'll still be there?"

She laughed, happy with his anxiety. "As Sally would tell you, 'She can't go very far with a twisted ankle.'" Then, more seriously she added, "Yes, of course, I'll be here—waiting."

"Till tomorrow then," he said quietly.

"Till tomorrow," she answered wistfully, and she heard the receiver click.

She leaned her head back and closed her eyes. He missed her!

"Here's your herbal tea," the booming voice said, as Sally placed a tray on the table next to Tracy's elbow. In her reverie Tracy never even heard Sally; she nearly had to be scraped from the ceiling.

100

"Good grief, Sally, I didn't hear you—you scared me."

"Made enough noise, but you seemed to be day-dreaming. Here, I made little tea sandwiches for you. Your father said to make sure you eat something. Oh, yes, and dinner will be at seven sharp."

"I'm not going anywhere," Tracy said playfully, looking beneath the bread to see what goodies were stashed there. "Oh, chicken and cheese. But I'll never eat dinner if I eat these."

"Well, you'd better; you need your strength to get better. Remember, the doctor is coming to-morrow."

"To look at my ankle, not my stomach. But," she relented, "maybe just one."

"That's better," the massive creature smiled, and she patted Tracy on the head with her wooden spoon. As she walked from the room, she called over her shoulder, "So, it wasn't one of the little guys, eh?" There was a decided snicker as she headed for her pots and pans.

The following day the doctor advised Tracy that she was doing fine, and she should be up and around in two days. She was thrilled. By midday Tracy was a nervous wreck, wishing that evening would come. She picked up her book—again—but the words didn't seem to make any sense. Then she spied Scotty cutting across the lawn. She hadn't seen him since Mark had called so she hadn't had a chance to reprimand him for his little lapse of memory.

"Hi, lass," the familiar voice called. "Just saw the Doc; says you'll be up and around in a couple of days. That's great, 'cause I've got some great news for you." He walked over and squatted down before her. "Guess what?" he teased.

101

"You forgot to tell me I received a phone call." She crossed her arms across her chest defensively.

"What? A phone call? No. *I* received a phone call." He dismissed her question with his outstretched hand. "How would you like to strut your stuff down in Hialeah?"

"Florida?" She leaned forward enthusiastically. "The very place . . ."

"That's wonderful," Tracy exclaimed. "When?"

"Next week, my lovely, so get better fast." Then he stood up and took her hand in his. "You look great to me, but make sure you stay off that foot."

"That foot," she assured him, "hasn't touched carpet in five days." And she leaned back. "Florida —just think. Oh, I can't wait." Tracy looked down at her foot and wiggled her toes. "Get better, foot, quickly. We are going to ride at Hialeah!" She turned her head to Scotty, who was leaning and looking out the window.

"What a day, lass. But we'll have just as good down there—if not better." He turned to face her, his hands in his pockets. "You're making quite a name for yourself; I'm proud of you."

She was playing with the corner of her book and added, "Only because I've such a good trainer."

"You'd do great without me, lass, but thanks anyway. Listen, I'm going to have Sally rustle me up a sandwich. You want anything?"

And as he headed for the doorway, Tracy didn't look up from her book, but asked quietly, "Why didn't you tell me Mark Flanagan called the other day?"

"Oh, didn't I? Must have told Sally and she forgot . . ." He was out of the room and down the hall.

But Tracy was so elated with the news that she

dismissed the concern of the phone call and concentrated on the upcoming events. She was going to ride in Florida and Mark was coming tonight. She leaned over to pick up her crutches and headed toward the bathroom and her pink-and-white scale. Just because you're resting, doesn't mean you shouldn't weigh yourself in, she told herself. She put her weight on her left leg and very slowly lowered the right leg. It didn't hurt—but what she saw did! One hundred and nine pounds. She moaned, closed her eyes, and looked again. There it was—109! No mistake—she had gained four pounds. She quickly grabbed her crutches and hobbled back to her lounge. This would never do; she couldn't be more than 105 if she expected to ride in Hialeah. Tracy swung herself expertly onto the seat, released herself from the crutches, and tossed them across the room in a fit of temper. She took several deep breaths and made a resolution. She'd lose the extra pounds, and lose them quickly. She was going to ride at Hialeah, and she was going to meet her riding weight!

When Scotty peeked his head in and asked, "Sure you don't want some of this?" He pointed to a thick roast beef sandwich on his plate, and she quickly replied, "I'm sure." You don't know how sure, she thought.

Eight o'clock arrived and still no Mark. Give him time, he has to make his way from the airport. She stirred, hearing her father's movements in the hall.

"How's my girl?" he asked entering the room and looked down at her lovingly.

"Fine, fine." She smiled up at him.

He sighed heavily, patted her head, and looked into her face questioningly. "You okay, Trace?"

His face registered concern as he chewed on his cigar. "You hardly ate at all at dinner—just some tomatoes and onions."

"Just wasn't hungry, Pop. Guess I'm just anxious to be up and around and to ride down in Florida."

"Are you sure that's all?" He paused, waiting for a reply. When there was none, he added enthusiastically, "You'll do just fine; you'll make me proud." He leaned over and kissed her forehead.

"Knowing you're there behind me, Bull,"—she winked—"will certainly make me feel better."

"Well, then, as long as that's all, and you're sure you'll be all right, I'll run along. And, don't forget," he added, lighting the end of his burned-out cigar, "Sally's upstairs if you need her. Just ring the bell; she'll hear you." He smiled in the direction of the little bell Scotty had brought her in case she needed anything. He stopped and looked at her. "So"—he stroked his prominent chin—"Mark Flanagan's stopping by to see you, is he? That's nice. Sorry, I'll miss him. He's got a filly I'm interested in, but—well, another time." At the mention of his name, Tracy nervously adjusted her new aqua blouse that accentuated her bright emerald eyes.

"Yes," she said, "he's stopping by . . . if he gets the chance."

"Well, I'll be off, then." He leaned over and kissed her on the cheek. "Don't be too anxious, baby. A few more days and you'll be in that saddle. Just relax."

At 8:30, the doorbell rang, and Tracy could hear Sally's mellifluous bellow, "Okay, okay, I'm coming—hold on. Give a body a chance."

"Hi." Tracy could hear his voice. "I'm Mark Flanagan. I've come to see Tracy."

"Yep," she said, closing the door, "I know who you are and why you've come. Well," she said with a sigh, "at least you're big."

Tracy cringed. On the plus and minus scale, Sally was logging up a lot of minuses.

"Follow me," she commanded. They walked down the carpeted corridor. "Well, there she is," Sally said.

"Thank you." He paused, then he smiled and added, "Sally."

"No trouble." She dabbed at her straggly hair. "You just ring if you need anything, Tracy. I'm going upstairs to watch TV."

"Fine, Sal. Thanks."

Mark crossed the room in two long strides and stared down at her. His hair was windblown and his tie was askew.

Tracy looked up at him. "She is the only person in the world who intimidates me." Her heart was racing. Could it be possible? Was he even more handsome than she remembered?

"I don't believe that," he said, looking at her longingly. Then he walked a little farther and stared down at her foot. "Umm, not bad, not bad . . ."

"You don't have a foot fetish, do you?"

"Not the last time I checked," he said with a smile. "But with you I could probably develop one." She returned his smile. He leaned over, kissed her forehead, and whispered in her ear, "Do you think there's enough room on that chaise to allow me to rest these weary bones? I'm bushed."

"Oh sure, sure," she said and wiggled a few inches to the right, allowing him sufficient space to sit. As he did, his leg brushed against hers, and he

105

pressed closer to her. He took both her hands in his.

"Tracy," he whispered, and his deep-set eyes said it all.

"Mark." She answered in a weak voice. They stared for a while, and all the time he stroked her hand.

"Well"—he cleared his throat and pointed at the ankle—"it doesn't look too bad. In fact, it looks pretty good." And he turned back to face her. "Trace, you look wonderful and healthy."

"I look wonderful and fat!"

"Fat?" He looked at her unbelievingly.

"Yes." She extended her lower lip in mock concern. "I've gained a . . ." she hesitated and added, "couple of pounds."

"That'll disappear as soon as you're up and around," he said. "Besides, you could stand a few pounds; you're not exactly the world's greatest eater." He squeezed her hand. "You know, you had me very worried. You've got to take better care of yourself. You're so independent. No one can tell you anything . . ."

"Believe me, Mark, I didn't go looking for that rock," she added, annoyed. "This is not my idea of enjoyment, or a way of getting attention. And, I might add, you sound just like my father." She took a deep breath. "Anyway, you're always running off all over the country, doing what you please, seeing whoever you please . . ."

"Hey, Tracy, back off. I'm very concerned about you." He let go of her hand, loosened his tie, and opened his shirt. Before she could continue, he put his finger to her busy lips. "Settle down. There's no reason for such an outburst. I'm just worried."

The glow from the lamp made shadows dance

across his rugged features, and she found his eyes disarmingly inviting. What were they arguing about anyway? He was the best medicine for her, and he definitely sent her temperature soaring.

"If you're worried, then I'm glad," she said sensually.

He caressed the side of her face, and she raised her hand to touch his. They were silent for a few minutes, their eyes saying it all. She could feel his hot breath on her face, and she felt herself coloring. Her lips parted, and he whispered close to her mouth, "Tracy . . ."

She lowered her eyes and slipped her arms around his neck.

"Stop talking so much and kiss me," she implored heatedly.

"You're a demanding little wench." He lowered his head to accommodate her. "I've been wanting to do this since I've walked in the room."

First his full, sensuous lips just brushed hers tenderly, and then he moistened his lips and began to caress her beckoning mouth with tiny kisses. Slowly his tongue invaded her mouth. At first he was gentle, but as the passion was aroused within him, his kiss became more brutal. He slid his arms around her slim back and lifted her slightly and pressed himself to her. His kiss was so fierce, so demanding, that she started to gasp. He released her slowly and her head tilted back, and he ran his strong fingers through her hair. Tiny moans escaped through her moistened lips, and her dark lashes fluttered above sensual, half-closed eyes.

Then his strong hand left her hair and slid down her cheek, across her trembling lips to her milky throat and then, ever so slowly, it worked its way inside the low-cut blouse. His fingers were inside her lacy bra, playing, teasing. He stared at her, breathing heavily, and she moaned slightly. "Mark, I . . ."

"Quiet, you devil. I just want to look at you." His voice was so gruff, so harsh, that it only served to arouse her more. Her head rolled back and forth while she sighed, and his hand worked itself farther and farther inside her bra. Tracy's nipple was hard and incredibly sensitive to his touch. She wanted him so badly she thought she'd burst. His mouth sought hers again. "Tracy, Tracy," he cried. "I've missed you so." His voice was husky with emotion.

"Oh, Mark, I've been so unhappy." She squeezed her arms around his neck tighter and brought him closer to her. Her lips parted and her tongue ran over his lips, teasing, demanding, forcing his mouth to open and receive her tongue. He met her demands, and then he pulled his mouth from hers and looked into the sultry eyes and allowed his tongue to play with her neck. Down, down, his tongue led a path over her throat, deeper, until it buried itself between her hot, heaving breasts. Tracy bit her lip in an attempt to stifle her cries. She moaned, finally, and said in a low, throaty voice, "Oh, Mark . . ."

Slowly, he pulled away from her; his hands and mouth reluctantly left her swollen breasts. He could hardly speak. "This is crazy, senseless—not here, not with Sally . . ."

She cut him off and brought her mouth again to his, moistening her lips. "Let Sally get her own man!" And she kissed him passionately. They were locked together motionless for a long moment as Mark returned her fiery kiss, his tongue relentless as he explored her mouth. Tracy reached up and pushed her fingers through his thick, brown hair, and then caressed the back of his neck. Finally, her nails dug into his skin passionately, and now it was his turn to groan, and her name exploded from his lips. "Tracy, Tracy, we've got to stop . . ." Slowly, he pulled away from her. He sat back and pushed his hand through his hair, leaned over and straightened her blouse with his free hand. He stood up. He was going to be sensible for both of them; she could feel it coming. With his back to her, he said, "Not here—not like this; we're not alone. It's just that I couldn't wait to see you, and . . ."

"I know, I know," she whispered. She took a very deep breath and added, "I understand." There was a lengthy pause while he stared out the window, and she stared at his back. Finally, she leaned over and turned up the radio. Then she broke the silence. "I'm sure sorry I sprained my ankle."

He turned to her and smiled. "So am I." There was another pause. "When will you be up and around?"

"Two days probably."

There was another pause while he just held her hand. Then he cleared his throat and attempted to continue the conversation. He was perspiring heavily. "You're not going to ride right away, are you? I mean, you need to rest and . . ."

"Please, don't say it—don't say relax. I don't think I ever want to hear that word again."

"No, no, I was going to say, be careful with that ankle. After all, you don't want to make it worse by riding too quickly."

It was difficult trying to make small talk when they were both so physically aroused, Tracy thought, but she had to try. She fluffed up her pillow, made herself comfortable, and looked up at him. "I promise I'll take care of myself."

"Good." He turned to her. "Then suppose I take you on your first day—on your own two feet—over to my place. I'd like to show you a two-year-old colt that I just bought."

"You?" She raised a curious eyebrow.

"Yes, I figure since I'm going to be in the business—for a while anyway—I might as well get my feet wet. Believe me"—he smiled at her—"I didn't do it alone; I had a lot of help. My trainer, Wally, and my foreman, Fred, spotted him when they were in Virginia, and when I saw him, he looked great to me." He moved closer and looked down at her. "So," he pushed his hands deep into his pockets and rocked slightly, "now I guess I'm one of the horsey set."

"Congratulations." She beamed. "So, that's why you ran out on me." She winked and patted the empty space beside her. "Come, sit down."

"Tracy, I think I'd best stay here, I feel safer somehow."

She laughed. "Perhaps you're right. I only wanted to tell you that in a week I'll be riding down in Hialeah. Isn't that great?"

"Great." His smile disappeared and he looked at the ceiling. "How long will you be away—any idea?"

"Probably a week or two. Why don't you fly down to see me?"

"Maybe I just might. But"—one hand worked to the back of his neck and he walked around the room—"but I've got a lot of things to do here. I might not be able to make it."

"All right, we'll leave it at maybe."

"Right, maybe it is." He sat down beside her. "I'd better be going, Spitfire. I'm done in—and you're not safe to be around."

"Oh, I hope not." She slipped her hands around his neck and pulled his head toward hers. She brought her mouth to his again and kissed him hard, then pushed him away. "That's till two days from now."

"You *are* a witch," he whispered, and he bolted to his feet.

"Doc is going to see me late tomorrow afternoon to give me a clean bill of health." She smiled up at the rugged face.

"I'll call you tomorrow night then and pick you up the next morning—if you're *clean,*" he teased. "Now I have to run."

"Coward," she yelled to his retreating back.

"You know it," he called over his shoulder.

He threw her a kiss and went down the hall. She heard the door close behind him.

Tracy turned off her lamp and started to undress in the dark; the stream from the moonlight afforded her sufficient light. A familiar growl filled the den, and Tracy rubbed her empty stomach. She resisted the urge to hop to the kitchen; she had only eaten a few vegetables all day, and she wasn't going to ruin her track record now. In a few days she would be back to her riding weight of 105. She was determined. She fell asleep hungry, but content, with the vision of Mark's smiling face before her.

"Well," the doctor said, pushing his chubby hands against his stubby legs and raising himself, "you've obviously obeyed my orders. That ankle is as good as new."

111

"You mean I can get up and actually stand—all by myself?"

"Yes—but no tight riding boots for you for two days. Give it a chance, Tracy." Then he shook his head. "Heaven knows, I could've used you on The Cricket the other day; I lost fifty bucks on that filly."

"Sorry, Doc." Tracy smiled, slowly swinging her legs over the chaise and standing up. She stretched her arms toward the ceiling. "Ah, it feels great to stand; I was beginning to get bed sores—or rather—lounge sores."

"Well, we seem pretty chipper and none the worse for wear. Guess you won't be needing me anymore . . ."

Tracy whirled and put her hands on his shoulders and looked at him. "Tell you what I'm gonna do, Doc," she said with a wink. "I'll bring in a winner—my first mount. Give you a chance to get your money back."

"Guarantee?" He winked back.

"With horses?" She laughed. "You know better than that; but I promise you I'll do my best." She removed her hands.

"That's good enough for me," he said and turned and picked up his black bag. "Now remember, little lady, go slow and no more tripping."

"Promise, Doc." She spun around.

"Well"—he squinted his eyes impishly—"I've treated people for sprained ankles before, but none of them exhibited your elation or reaction. Have I developed the Midas touch—or do I detect a much deeper source for your happiness?"

"Now, now, Doc, leave the delving to the Freudians." She peeked from behind her long hair. "I can ride. That's why I'm so ecstatic. And while I'm at it, I'll bring you in a winner."

"I should have known better than to ask," he said, walking toward the door. "Women—especially women jockeys and especially *this* woman jockey!" His sprightly walk took him through the door quickly.

Tracy yelled; "I'll see you around the paddock, Doc."

The rest of the afternoon Tracy spent outdoors around the stables talking to the assistant trainers and grooms. They were all glad to see her up and about, and Tracy felt great—but hungry. She stayed away from Sally's kitchen.

That night Mark called and told her he would pick her up at nine in the morning. Tracy slept in her own bed—the first time in days—and she felt refreshed the following morning.

She made herself a weak herbal tea and waited for him on the front steps as he pulled up.

"Hi," she jumped into the car, closing the door behind her and holding the tea in her Styrofoam cup.

"Hi, yourself," he returned, and eased the car down the curving driveway, giving her a sidelong glance. When he was outside her property, he pulled the car to the side of the road and leaned over without saying a word and kissed her—at first tenderly, and then more passionately. She returned the kiss warmly, excited by his touch.

When he finally released her, she spoke in a low voice, looking into the wistful eyes. "Thanks, I needed that."

He smiled, started the engine, and pulled out on the road. Some tea spilled from her cup. "Oops." She dabbed at her jeans with a tissue. "The

113

hazards of passion." And she continued to sip her tea.

"Is that breakfast?" He pointed to the cup.

"No, no, Sally fixed me something earlier," she lied. Then she looked at him askance. He was incredibly handsome, she thought, in a blue-and-white striped shirt and new jeans. Tracy decided he was a challenge to any woman, and she was going to accept that challenge. How she had missed him. They fell silent for a while and then he turned to her.

"You look . . ."

"Please," she stopped him, "don't say healthy."

"No, no, I won't," he said. "I was going to say, if you had let me finish"—and he turned to her and gave her that wonderful, engaging smile—"that you look radiant, you know." He paused. "Full of life."

Next I'm sure I'll hear, "bouncy," she thought. "Well, you try staying indoors under the auspices of Sally, the personality kid, and see if you're not full of life when you're let out. I feel as if I've been released—on probation, though. Can't ride yet; that is, my foot will not see a boot for two days, when I have my first mount. Can't wait," she said with a sigh and put her head back on the leather seat.

"Yes, I guess for you to be inactive is . . ."

"Like receiving a sentence," she finished for him.

He laughed and turned on the radio. "I thought you might like to see my place and take a look at that colt we bought."

"I'd love to." She looked at him and could see pride showing on his face. They fell silent again, and Tracy felt an electricity between them that was almost disquieting.

Fifteen minutes later they approached a huge white Colonial house surrounded by large pines and well-manicured shrubbery. He left the driveway and continued around to the back of the house and parked on the gravel beneath an immense oak. The stables were to the left and stretched well into the back of his acreage. The sun was cutting a path through the many trees that lined the property, affording shade over the red-and-white stables. It was a scene of understated elegance.

"Not much, but we call it home, right?" she teased. "Mark, it's beautiful."

"Come on, I'll show you around." He squeezed her hand and then reached across her and opened her door. His warm body lightly touching hers sent shivers through her.

They walked around the grounds and headed behind the stables. Tracy spied a white bungalow off to the right about fifty yards from the house.

"What's that?" She pointed in the direction of the small house.

"Oh, that—that's the old guest house that I told you I had turned into my workshop. I'm afraid there's just a lot of wood and blueprints and sawdust. In a word—a mess. I guess I'm just a frustrated inventor, still searching to design that new, slim, affordable sailboat and hoping some enterprising manufacturer will recognize my genius and buy my designs—" He laughed nervously.

"Could I see it later?" she interrupted.

He looked down at her, noticing the genuine interest in her upturned face.

"My workshop, you mean? I'm afraid there isn't

much to see—just a workroom, a tiny kitchen, and a small sitting room with some dated furniture." He stopped. "It does have one redeeming feature, though; it has a fireplace—and it works. But, I haven't had it going for some time, not since . . ." He paused, and a dark shadow crossed his face. Maybe it wasn't right, he thought, bringing someone else here so soon. Soon? After all this time? Snap out of it. Besides, this bundle of energy wasn't just another someone.

"Well," he continued, swallowing, "not since I've been away all these months. But, come, I want to show you my pride and joy." He brightened. He took her hand and Tracy felt warm all over.

She had noticed the awkward pause in his dialogue, but she said nothing. Mark Flanagan was going to have to disperse his own ghosts. "Great," she said and looked up at him. "Let's look at this precious colt." They walked toward the stall, and Tracy was aware of the heat from his body as he slipped his strong arm around her waist.

As they approached the stall, he released her, went inside, and led the colt out by the reins. The horse veered and raised its head, giving off a loud neigh. Tracy looked up, watching the sunlight dance across the mahogany back. "Why, he's beautiful, Mark." Instinctively, she grabbed the reins. Now the horse whinnied as if in assent to the transmittal of hands. Tracy held the reins loosely and walked alongside the horse, patting its shiny coat and talking softly to it. "You are a beauty," she said as she rubbed his underbelly. The horse whinnied again, flapping the loose reins around him and turned its head to look at the new tender, loving hands caressing him.

"I think he approves of you," Mark said, leaning

against a tree. He was chewing, very sensuously, Tracy noticed, on a piece of straw, his teeth biting intermittently, on the dry weed. The sun danced over his hair and face, causing disparate shadows to form. He pushed the straw to the corner of his mouth and moistened his lips with his tongue.

Tracy tossed her head back and swallowed. "And if he does," she added, lowering her eyes sensuously, "then the feeling is mutual." She turned from Mark and continued patting and talking to the horse as it turned its head around and around in a circle and emanated a contented, low whinny.

"You have him eating out of your hand; he's acting like a pussycat instead of next year's derby winner," he said drolly. His arms leaned across his opened shirt, and his highly polished cordovan boots crossed at the ankle. He was eyeing her hungrily, still chewing the straw.

She took a deep breath and returned his stare with raised eyebrows. "Next year's derby, eh?" she said and stepped back from the horse, appraising him. "He just might, he just might," she mused. Tracy tucked in her shirt and dried her perspiring palms on her jeans. His eyes traveled over her body greedily, making no attempt to hide his passion. "Well," Tracy said and coughed, "what's— what's his name?" She could feel the blotches surfacing on her warm chest.

"Well"—he stroked his jutting chin—"he was sired by Winged Victory; I thought maybe Pegasus would be a good choice."

Her hair flung around her shoulders as she turned to him. He was smiling and still chewing. Did he remember, she wondered, their first meeting when she had mentioned that she rode around

117

her father's estate as if on the wings of Pegasus—or was it just a coincidence? But the smile confirmed what she wanted to believe. Then she dropped the reins and took a few steps toward him. "Could I ride him, Mark—could I ride your Pegasus?" she asked. She grabbed the reins and pulled the horse behind her. Her blouse tightened across her breasts and he stared at her full bosom.

He finally pushed himself away from the tree, and, very determinedly, walked toward her. "I thought the doctor said—"

"He said not in a boot," she cut him off, and pointed down to her relatively soiled boaters. "Come on, Mark, you know how doctors are—and I won't take no for an answer."

She looked at him defiantly, tossed her hair from her shoulders, and moistened her lips tantalizingly. Her eyes were alive, a deep sparkling green against her creamy skin. Her cheeks were ablaze with anticipation.

Looking the way she did, he knew he could refuse her nothing. He relented. "Okay, have it your own way—but not too long."

"Great, let's saddle him up," she said and raced inside the stall. His eyes followed her as she turned, drawn by the full breasts and slim waist. Mark knew he was devouring her every move, and the more he did, the more aroused he became. He kicked at a stone and resignedly followed her and brought out the saddle.

When the horse was ready, she smiled bewitchingly. "Give me a leg up?"

He cupped his hands and she was astride Pegasus in a shot, looking down at him, her hair cascading around her shoulders, her eyes inviting. "By the way," she leaned over, her face very close to his, "where is everybody?" A curious glint lit the teasing green eyes.

"My foreman is taking care of some business for me today. The others won't be back till after three this afternoon." He kept his hand on her thigh, and she looked down at him.

"Oh," she said simply, a smile coming to her lips. She pulled back on the reins, and he removed his hand. Pegasus lifted his front legs. "Come on, boy, let's go," she exclaimed, and Tracy lowered her head into the horse's neck to avoid the low trees. They headed for the open fields, clearing the first fence with distance to spare.

"Be careful . . ." Mark called, knowing his words would be completely unheeded. He watched as the horse cantered, and then broke into a trot. Tracy turned once, waved to him, and shouted, "Fantastic!" Then she galloped off once more into the distance. Mark leaned across the fence and watched her as she flew across his property. She looked about sixteen years old with her hair flailing around her—her exuberance giving life to the horse. He sighed and watched, and his heart beat faster. She and Pegasus moved in unison, and her movements were fluid and graceful. She was provocative—the tight jeans hugging her muscular thighs as she guided the horse expertly, set off by the trim hips and tiny waist. And the more he observed, the more heated he became. He could still taste the sweetness of her lovely mouth. How he wanted her; and he knew he would have her soon.

He motioned for her to return. She finally relented and rode toward him, faster and faster, heading for the fence at the end of the stables, her breasts straining against the material of her shirt.

"Tracy," he yelled, "take it easy, no jumping." But it was too late; his command fell on deaf ears, and she hurdled the wooden fence.

"Tracy . . ." he yelled, red-faced, as she trotted toward him, panting, "you could've been hurt riding that recklessly. I don't care if you are a professional. You don't know that horse and you took too many chances." But she wasn't listening; she was leaning over, her face flushed, next to the horse's ear, complimenting him on a great ride. She pulled up next to Mark and slid from the horse. She was sweating, her eyes wide with excitement, her cheeks red from the wind.

"He's a beauty," she panted, catching her breath. "C'mon, let's walk him a bit to cool him down." And Mark couldn't help but wonder who was going to walk *him* to cool him down. The prospect made him smile.

They walked silently, one on either side of Pegasus. Finally, Tracy said, "Okay, you can put him back now." And she handed Mark the reins; she was still short of breath.

He locked the gate behind the animal and walked toward her. She was leaning with her back to the fence, supporting herself with her elbows, watching his deliberate steps as he came toward her. She was looking at his tight, new jeans that so clearly showed the muscles in his legs and at his shirt, opened at the top exposing the dark hair of his chest.

He was eyeing her, too. Her hair was matted against her forehead and there was a vibrant glow to her cheeks. The sound of her erratic breathing stirred him, and he stopped in front of her to face her squarely. He placed his hands on her shoulders firmly and could feel her hot, sweaty body beneath

120

his grip. He was burning up inside and his mouth was dry. Finally, he released her shoulders and took her by the hand, saying nothing. Quietly, he led her toward the back of the barn.

Pushing her inside an unused stall, he closed the half door behind him, and pressed her gently against the weather-stained wood. He ran his fingers through her auburn hair. Then, he let his right index finger touch the soft skin of her cheek, caress her quivering lips, run beneath her chin, and then down her slim throat. She shuddered as his hand went lower still, until he touched her breast. "You could've been hurt," he said, his voice low and sensual, and he allowed his other hand to slip around her waist. He could feel her body burning beneath the light material of her blouse. She was hot—as hot as he—he knew it.

"But I wasn't," she murmured through partly opened lips, "and I do love it—It excites me . . ."

"I know you do." His mouth opened, and his tongue played teasingly along his teeth. "And if it's thrills and excitement you want, then . . ." He didn't need to finish! He simply bent his head down toward hers, and with half-closed eyes, his mouth slowly opening wider, his lips closed over hers hungrily. Then he pushed her down, overcoming her feeble resistance, until she was on the floor, almost engulfed in a small pile of clean hay. Her chest was heaving and she saw the fire in his eyes. The scent from her heated body, mixed with her perfume, was driving him crazy. He began unbuttoning her blouse.

"Oh, Mark—someone might . . ." She half-pleaded.

"I told you no one was coming back till after

121

three. I need you and I want you *now.*" He gasped, "I've waited too long!"

There was an urgency to his voice that frightened Tracy, but soon his mouth was smothering hers, and she could do nothing but return his fiery passion with her own. He pushed her further into the hay and pressed his body on top of hers. One hand was inside her shirt, and with the other hand he pulled down the zipper of her jeans and let his fingers play over her taut stomach.

She was aching for him, but she kept thinking of where they were. And as he clung to her, she moaned, "But Mark . . ." His mouth silenced her and only muffled groans could be heard as she writhed beneath him. Slowly, he raised himself from her and removed her shoes. Then he tenderly slid the jeans down past her slim hips. He gasped when he saw the hot glow of her body. She finished opening her shirt, as her misty eyes returned his lingering look. They stared at each other, he lifted her and unclasped her bra and tossed it aside. She could object no longer.

She lay before him motionless as he lowered himself onto her. "Just waiting to be mounted, aren't you?" he asked in a gruff voice. Her arms closed tightly around him as if she were hungry to devour him. He pressed his massive chest and muscular thighs against hers. His breathing was labored and he blurted out, "Tracy, Tracy—my wild, uncontrollable filly—I've got to have you." His arms encompassed her and his tongue was inside her mouth. She returned his passion as their bodies merged.

Tracy felt it was better than the first time—but how could she be certain? She couldn't even think —she was being tossed into a distant galaxy, and a

122

black velvety sensation enveloped her. She was drifting, drifting—never to return—and then he broke the spell; a voice was calling her back.

"Tracy, Tracy; you'll drive me crazy . . . Tracy . . ." he exploded, "Tracy, I love you!"

And Tracy knew she'd never again experience such ecstasy—such happiness. All she could mumble through swollen, burning lips was, "Oh, Mark, I love you—I love you, too." And they held each other as warm, rapturous waves washed over them. They were oblivious to their surroundings and engulfed in their own emotions. And now they were both committed.

CHAPTER SIX

Hialeah was warm and sunny with clusters of palm trees dotting the track. Tracy was enjoying the weather and the acclaim; she had won two races out of five her first day, and she was basking in the accolades attributed to her expert riding style by the Press. She was also becoming aware of the jealousy exhibited by some of the veteran jockeys.

"Don't get excited, lass," Scotty was saying, "they're just testin' your mettle, so to speak. You're in a tough game—there's *mucho dinero* at stake. It's a competitive game; you're going to work for that popularity out there."

So, the following day, Tracy worked for it. As they came around the last turn, one of the top jockeys, Martinez, pushed Tracy to the outside, making her swing wide, losing ground. She let him pass her, and when there was a tiny opening, switched her whip from her left to right hand and beat Lacey's Dream across the rump, guiding him through the break toward the rail. There was an opening, and she buried her head in the horse's neck and hugged the rail hard, all the while urging her horse on with her whip. The horse next to her was losing speed, but she could see that Martinez was still coming on strong on Heart's Delight.

"C'mon, Lacey baby," she screamed in the

horse's ear, "don't let him beat us—don't!" She was making herself as light as she could. She was out of the saddle and as far up on the horse's neck as was possible. "Another inch and you'll be wearing me like a hat," Tracy yelled at the horse as they went flying over the finish line.

The announcer was screaming through the mike: *And that's it, ladies and gentlemen; Lacey's Dream inches out Heart's Delight by a nose. And —that is some ridin', ladies and gentlemen. A mile and a sixteenth in a minute and forty-five. That little lady can ride . . .*

The following day the papers sang Tracy's praises in the Sports headlines: "Morgan Miffs Martinez," "Tracy Wins on Lacey," "Tracy's Dream Overrules Martinez's Heart," and so on.

Tracy snuggled beneath the covers and sipped her tea, feeling smug and successful. The sun was dancing in uneven patches across the blue-green rug as she stared out the hotel window. It was a huge room and she felt like a princess—without her prince. They were going into their second week and Mark still couldn't break away. Her lower lip protruded, and she raised her knees to accommodate her chin. She allowed a heavy sigh to escape and then threw off the covers and headed for the shower. She slipped off her robe and stepped on the scale. One hundred and three; her starvation tactics were paying off. But as she stood in the shower letting the warm water run down her body, she admitted that she was having more and more difficulty keeping food down—any food of substance. She was all right if she picked . . .

The phone rang and Tracy yelled instinctively,

"Just a minute!" She turned off the taps, grabbed a towel, and ran to the phone.

"Hello," she said, out of breath.

"You weren't putting your horse through its paces in the room, were you?" the droll voice asked.

"Mark, is that you?"

"None other . . ."

"No, no, I just ran from the shower to answer . . ." She sat down on the bed holding her towel securely around her chest with her free hand. Her feet formed two wet imprints on the cushiony rug. She played with her toes as he talked. His resonant voice always sent shivers up and down her spine. She wondered if it would always do that to her. He was continuing.

". . . I don't want you to slip and break your neck—for a phone."

"No, no, I promise—not for a phone . . ." She paused, wallowing in the magic of his voice. He even thrilled her long distance! "Are you going to be able to come down; we'll be here another week." She squeezed her eyes shut, hoping the answer would be yes.

"Doesn't look that way, Sprite. I've been working pretty hard, and I've come up with a new design for my boat . . ."

"Oh, I see," she said in a tiny, disappointed voice and allowed the towel to drop. Thinking how funny it was that people adhered to such a stringent code of modesty when talking alone on the phone, she picked up the towel and again fastened it around her.

"But I've been reading and hearing some fantastic things about you."

Tracy drew her head up from where it had been

settling, dejectedly on her chest, and cleared her throat. In the back of her mind the old familiar cliché of her father's about keeping her heart on her sleeve struck her. She certainly wasn't going to beg him to come down if he was too busy, but how she longed for him. She could picture his strong arms cradling her and the rough texture of his fingers stroking her breasts until she thought she'd explode. His deep voice brought it all back. She ached for him. She turned her thoughts back to the conversation.

"Have you now?" she replied. "Then maybe you should come down and find out for yourself," she added in her most seductive voice.

"If I could, I would," he said. "But I can't. I just wanted to call to tell you that I miss you, and how proud I am of you. You're racking up quite a score for yourself."

"This is not a tennis match," she quipped.

"I know. It's the sport of kings." He laughed. "And, you are all over the Sports pages. You should be excited."

"I am," she snapped, "but I'd like to share that excitement with *someone*—not everyone!" Suddenly, Tracy felt very testy. He sounded so close that she was hot and bothered. But this telephone was keeping them apart and she was frustrated. She rubbed her fingers over the top of her breasts and bit her lip. You always seem to have enough time for *your* business, she was huffing, to work on your boats and to travel all over the place, but you can't seem to spare the time for me. "You're right," she yelled, "it would have been a perfect day, *if* you had been there!"

There was a long pause on the other end; this conversation was not taking the turn he had expected. "Tracy," he said coolly, and with determination, "we both knew we couldn't be together for a while. We discussed this last time."

But the picture of their raw, frenzied lovemaking was immediately projected on a screen in her mind. She swallowed and stroked her chest, which, she noticed, was all blotchy.

"Yes, yes," she interjected hurriedly. She was being a little too cryptic with her remarks, but she was irritable, and it was difficult to control her temper. "I know we did—I guess I just wanted to have you with me. Oh, damn," she said, letting her breath escape heavily.

Another pause, and a more gentle voice asked, "Have you calmed down, Trace?"

More air expelled. "Not really, but what can I do with all these miles between us? Damn!"

"You said that," he said with a laugh. Then, more seductively, he whispered into the phone, "I'll make it up to you, Trace—I promise. There'll be *nothing* between us . . ."

And Tracy thought her towel would catch on fire—his voice had such an effect on her. They were both quiet for a while, each remembering their last time together.

Mark broke the silence. "Let's change the subject; and speaking of being with you," he offered in a lighter tone, "in three weeks there will be a retirement dinner for Wally, my trainer. Would you care to join me?"

"Wally's retiring?" she asked. "I didn't know."

"Neither did I, till last week. So, will you accompany me, my spitfire?" Then he brightened. "And you know what?" Not waiting for her answer he continued, "That leaves a spot open for a top trainer for the Flanagan farms. Interested?"

"Who—me?" Her hand shot up to her Nefertiti medallion and she fingered it nervously. "What do you want to do? Retire me already? Why, I'm in my prime—or whatever—I'm finally doing just what I always wanted to do."

"All right, cease and desist—I was only teasing. But, you know, it is a thought—I mean, eventually. You'd make a great trainer . . ."

"I also, I understand, make a great *jockey*." She stood up abruptly, allowing the towel to drop to her feet. Oblivious to her nudity, and wearing it like a defiant badge, she strode around the room with the phone in one hand while the fingers of her other toyed with the long plastic cord.

"All right, back up, Trace, back up. I was only testing the waters—"

"Is your next line going to be, 'Let's run it up the flagpole and see who salutes it'?" She was flailing the air with the red phone as her left hand went unconsciously to her stomach. She was hungry, damn it, and unnerved. Then she was aware of the silence on the other end.

Despite himself, he laughed. "You are, without a doubt, unpredictable and one of a kind. And if I had you here, I'd put you over my knee. That temper . . ."

She replied in kind to his soothing tones, and attempted to remove all traces of hostility from her voice. "That wouldn't do my career much good, my little rump would be raw; you see, I'm parading around here in the nude . . ."

"Umm, I can picture that." He hesitated. "Tracy, I'm frantic . . ."

"Me, too," she confessed.

He let a long sigh escape and then added, "I'd

better hang up. You're driving me crazy. I can see you—and I need you . . ."

She heard the deep swallow on the other end, and she held the phone tightly to her breast, as if trying to bring him closer.

"Tracy, hurry home, I have no one to fence with—and no one who wears a towel quite the way you do . . ." His voice was low and husky.

At the sound of his throaty request, a cold shiver ran through her body. He had such a devastating effect upon her. She took a deep breath and replied, "I'll—I'll do my best to get home as quickly as possible; and Mark"—she smiled into the phone—"sorry I got angry. Guess I'm still a little edgy. What was the line my father used to tease my mother with? Oh, yes," she said, playing with her hair. "It's lonely at the top." But all this banter, she knew, did nothing to help the empty feeling she had whenever she was not with Mark.

"Somehow," he added, "I can picture your father saying that. But," he added huskily, "there's another picture that's forming in my mind, a much more lascivious one, so I'd better cut this conversation short."

"Yes, yes," she agreed, "and since it doesn't seem like you'll be paying me a visit down here, I'll leave you with this thought: I'm standing here in the nude, pining for you, too. Maybe that'll move you to hop a plane . . ."

"That's dirty pool, Trace." He paused. "I'll try, really I will, but if I can't, please rush home."

She missed him so much that it was sheer torment talking to him on the phone. Her body craved his embrace. She was actually sweating in her air-conditioned room.

"I'll—I will," she stammered and hung up.

Tracy returned to the shower and stayed there for a long, long time.

"Well, lass, you went down there, virtually unknown—"

"I beg your pardon?" She nudged her elbow playfully in Scotty's ribs as the big black limousine headed toward the Merritt Parkway and home.

"Well," he said with a smile, "let's put it this way: not as well known as you were up here. But, Trace, they were taken with you and you'll never have to worry about getting mounts down there. Ken said he had so many offers . . ." He paused and pointed to the trees lining the parkway. "Look, Trace, the leaves are beginning to turn," and he turned back to her. "Can't see that down in Florida now, can you?"

"No, no, you can't." And that's not the only thing that Florida couldn't offer, she thought. "I'm glad we're home, Scotty; as nice as it was, I'll have to admit I was getting a little homesick," and she laid her head back on the seat and thought of Mark.

The next few weeks were very busy, especially for Tracy, who was in demand as the leading apprentice jockey. She was enjoying her status. Mark was called away on business several times, and when they did see each other, there were always other people surrounding them. He, too, was developing a reputation for harboring quite a few top fillies and colts. He came a few times to see Bull Morgan and ask his help with a few problems.

By the time the retirement dinner came, Tracy was beside herself. It was a Saturday night, and she had ridden that afternoon and brought in a long shot. She had told Doc Olsen that she had a good

131

feeling about My Lovely Redhead—and she was right. It had won.

"Now do you forgive me, Doc?" she had teased.

"You can do no wrong as far as I'm concerned. I have, young lady, recouped my losses. Anytime you get those feelings, just give me a call."

"Why, Doc, you wouldn't want me to play favorites, would you?"

"Why not?" he answered. "That's what makes life interesting. You're one of my favorites," he said and winked. Then, as he started to walk away, he paused for a moment as if uncertain whether to add what was on his mind. He stroked his chin and thought for a moment.

"Trace? You feelin' okay? I mean, I noticed you've dropped a few pounds since I last saw you."

"Why, you old codger, you— Still looking at the young girls, eh?" Her attempt at levity didn't put him off.

"I notice *everything*, young lady . . ."

"Well," she interjected, "you want me to win, don't you? And you, above all, know my normal weight is slightly too heavy for a jockey. I've got to work to keep the pounds off. After all, Doc, fat jockeys don't bring in winners."

"Tracy, Tracy," he put his hand up in defense. "You don't have to tell me about a job I've been involved in all my life. The lady doth protest too much. I'm only asking. Are you eating enough?"

"Of course," she shot back haughtily, and a little too quickly, raising her head and brushing her hair aside. "It's just that I've been traveling and rushing, so . . ." She gave him her best smile.

"How much do you weigh?" he asked, assuming his professional voice. "No lies."

"About a hundred and three . . ."

132

"About? About? You who have to be weighed in every day—about? Come on, how much?"

"A hundred," she returned, kicking the dirt with her boot, "but"—she brought her head up enthusiastically—"I feel great!"

"As long as you're feeling all right; that's all I care about . . ."

"That and all the long shots I can bring in, right?"

"Yep. Well," he smiled amiably, "I can't stand here talking all day; I've got to get to my office."

Tracy waved to him and turned and walked back to the stables. Besides, she told herself, I really do feel great—well, most of the time, anyway.

Tracy sat down at her dressing table and put the afternoon's scenario out of her mind. She put on her favorite perfume and checked her new green silk, a low-cut dress that she had bought especially for tonight's festivities. Thank heaven, she didn't have to ride tomorrow. She was excited but exhausted, and she was looking forward to tonight and seeing Mark. In fact, she could think of nothing else! She pictured the familiar, handsome face, and his strong arms circling her waist, bringing her closer to him. She glanced at the clock and knew she'd be early and waiting for him; that's how fretful she was. Well, propriety be damned. She'd be on time. She craved those arms—that mouth—his hot body. And when he walked toward her with those long, purposeful strides, and his unruly, windblown hair, she thought she had never seen anyone so sexy in her life. And, he loved her! Tracy was on a high—living for the moment and loving it. No man had ever made her feel the way he did. She needed him.

In a state of nervous anxiety she slipped on her

dress. The soft lines followed the slim curves of her body exquisitely, and the color matched her eyes perfectly. Her mirror told her she looked a bit pale, but her new blush would fix that. She applied her make-up carefully and brushed her hair, but left it hanging loosely around her shoulders. No more sophisticated hairdos, she told her reflection. She stood back, swishing the layers of the skirt in her full-length mirror. Not bad for a lady "jock," she thought.

Voices drifted up from downstairs, and she knew Mark had arrived. She looked down and noticed her chest was all blotchy; it always did that when she was excited. Tracy took a few deep breaths and begged the blotches to disappear.

"You're conflicting with my green period," she told her chest.

She was all set, and realized she hadn't been this nervous the first time she rode out onto the track with thousands of people staring at her.

She headed for her door, then turned back to take a final look in her full-length mirror. Well, this is it, Trace ol' girl, and she headed for the stairs.

He was waiting for her at the bottom of the stairs looking very elegant in a dark suit, and Tracy wanted to tell him to forget dinner and run away. Instead, she smiled graciously, her heart thumping. He looked absolutely magnificent!

"Tracy" was all he said, and he led her to the car.

Once inside he turned to her as he started the engine. "No one would believe it." He eased out on the road.

"Believe what?" she asked.

"That—that body brought in a thirty-to-one long shot today."

"Does that mean you approve?" She smiled coyly.

"Oh, yes, indeed," he replied. "Yes, indeed."

"Then, can you *say* it?" she asked quietly.

He pulled off on a tiny side road and stopped the car. He turned to her and faced her squarely, the light from the street lamp reflecting an amber glow across his face.

"You look beautiful—gorgeous—okay?" He inched nearer.

"A good beginning anyway," she teased.

He leaned over and slid his arm beneath her coat, squeezed her to him, and tenderly put his lips on hers. Then the loving kiss turned more passionate, and she gasped.

"Please, Mark, don't—I mean, we'll never get to that dinner."

"It's your fault—you look so damned delectable —I'm only human." Resigned, he started the car and pulled onto the road.

"You were safe, though," he said, "that was my sweet and tender kiss." The tantalizing, crooked smile toyed at the corner of his mouth.

"Usually reserved for children and maiden aunts?" she queried.

"Not really, but I realize the wisdom of your statement; I'd better keep driving." He paused and then added casually, "Tracy—I know this is not your favorite topic, but beautiful as you are, you look a little too thin."

"You're right, this is definitely *not* my favorite subject. I'm fine; I've just been watching my weight, making sure I don't exceed . . ."

"Okay, okay," he said quickly and patted the slim hand on the seat. It was cold and she pulled away. He looked at her; he didn't want to spoil the

135

evening. "Okay, then prove it to me tonight. I hope I'm not going to be faced with a bowl full of chilled celery and tapered carrot sticks."

Even though she was annoyed, she laughed. "No, no, as a matter of fact, I'm hungry. A steak sounds good to me . . ."

"With a Caesar's salad?" He smiled at her and all the tenseness went out of her. She returned her hand to the seat, and he covered it with his.

"Yes. Oh, you, of the beautiful eyeteeth; with a Caesar's salad." She winked at him.

"You're a devil, and you've bewitched me, Tracy." He pulled into the parking lot of the restaurant, which was all ready half full.

"It's the green eyes that do it. Works every time; I weave this magic spell . . ."

He waved off the attendant, put a five-dollar bill in his hand, and parked the car himself.

"I take it you don't want to hear the squeal of burning rubber biting into offensive gravel, right?" she asked as he maneuvered between two Cadillacs.

"That—and this." He leaned over and cupped her face in his hands and stared at her with longing. Finally, after a long moment, he leaned over and kissed her hard and long. She moaned involuntarily. He released her, but said nothing.

Tracy's body was all aglow. She straightened the front of her dress. "You don't really *want* to go to this dinner, do you?"

His mood was broken, and he laughed and walked around to the passenger side of the car. He took her arm and lifted her to him as she alighted from the car. "In two minutes, if you don't stop, I'll cancel dinner and force you to take me somewhere and ravish me . . ."

"It's your fault"—he toyed with her ear—"for looking so ravishing."

"Touché." She pushed him away. "Let's go, Mark. I'm hungry."

"That's music to my ears," he said, and they walked hand in hand to the steps of the restaurant.

It was a very gala evening. A few speakers addressed Wally from the podium, and then dinner was served. There was a five-piece band and everyone was having a grand time.

Tracy ate an entire steak and part of her Caesar's salad. "See?" She leaned over. "No carrot sticks."

"I'll drink to that." He picked up his glass.

They drank and Tracy hummed with the music.

"Do you realize this is the first time we've been alone together—well, relatively alone?" He smiled. "Aside from the track, since you've returned from Hialeah?"

"As a matter of fact, I do." If you only knew how aware of that I am, she thought. She was staring at him while he talked, looking at the tiny gray hairs that were mixing with the brown at his sideburns, and the laugh creases that curled his lips, and the eyebrows that arched when he was excited. Tracy thought she had never seen anyone more handsome. She finally realized he was grinning widely at her—his drink poised.

"Tracy?"

"Oh, yes—yes— What?"

"I was just about to say that you would probably be arrested in Maine for wearing a dress like that."

"Oh, thank God." She beamed. "It was worn with full intent and forethought to arouse you. I thought I'd failed."

"Wench." He reached across the table and took

her hands. They smiled understandingly at each
other, happy just to touch.

"You look like a man who has something on his
mind, Mr. Flanagan." She sipped her drink, lowered
her eyes, and stretched across the table seductively,
her dress barely covering her breasts.

He stared at her for a long moment, unabashedly,
and then gulped his drink. "You are
something." He straightened in his chair and
Tracy smiled demurely, enjoying his discomfit. He
cleared his throat. "Well, to borrow your phrase,
'am I that transparent?'"

"No, but there's a look in your eye that I've
come to recognize. It's not," she whispered conspiratorially,
"a lewd look. It's more of an I-can't-
wait-to-tell-you look."

He squeezed her hand tighter. "Bright
girl . . ."

"And she rides, too." She returned the squeeze.
"I'm all ears."

"Well, I finished my latest design, and I've
mailed the blueprints to three manufacturers who
are interested. I should hear in three to four
weeks—"

"Oh, Mark," she interrupted, elated, "I'm so
happy for you."

"Well, don't get too excited; they have to accept
them, and there are always changes. But one firm I
spoke with in Rhode Island sounded very interested
and enthusiastic."

"That's great." Her eyes sparkled. "I just know
they'll want it. You know so much about boats.
But"—she paused—"why didn't you mention it
before—"

"Why?" he cut her off. "Why? You're harder to

reach than the President. We haven't exactly had a quiet conversation—"

"I know, I know," she interrupted. "But never mind, I'm thrilled for you. I know they'll want them," she said and she covered his hand with hers reassuringly.

"Thanks for the vote of confidence, but I feel you're a majority of one."

"Come on, defeatist, enough talk. How about finding some room on that crowded dance floor? My body is screaming to have your arms around me."

"I thought you'd never ask, hussy." He took her warm hand and guided her to the cramped dance floor.

It was crowded, but they attempted it anyway. He glided her around the floor, and she melted in his arms; for the first time in weeks she felt secure. She closed her eyes and tried to forget about all the other people around them and the boisterous talk that sailed above their heads. As they danced, it became noisier and warmer, and Tracy felt a bit dizzy. She looked up at him.

"Mark, do you think we could sit this one out?"

"It is a bit crowded," he agreed. He walked her back to their table and slipped the chair beneath her. "You're the most gorgeous woman jockey on the floor," he said in her ear.

"You've a reputation for saying that to all us jocks," she teased. But Tracy wasn't feeling in a teasing mood; she was feeling quite sick to her stomach. "Mark, would you excuse me for a minute?" She took her purse from the table.

"Sure, sure. Besides, I have to circulate a bit. Have to say hello to my new trainer, you know." Eddie Blake was an old-timer and a top trainer, and he had gladly accepted Mark's proposal to work for him.

Tracy walked, slightly unsteadily, to the ladies' room; at first slowly, then more quickly. Thankfully, no other women were in the room. She just made it in time. Then she ran cold water in the sink and patted her face with the wet toweling. She applied new make-up and smiled at herself in the mirror. She felt better, but not all that great. She walked, carefully, back to the table. She again began sweating.

Mark was still circulating, thank heavens. She sipped a cold drink and jumped when a hand tapped her on the shoulder.

"It's only me," he said, slipping into his seat. He poured himself some wine and looked at her. "Tracy, are you all right? You're as pale as a ghost . . ."

"You're not going to tell me I look worse than Hamlet's father, are you?" She smiled weakly. "That's been used."

"Stop it, Tracy," he said and reached for her hand. It was cold and clammy. Beads of perspiration were forming on her forehead, and her eyes were glassy and listless. He leaned nearer and said in a low voice, "Are you sure you're all right?" His other hand reached up and patted the side of her face. She was burning. "But, you're *not* all right, are you? You've been sick, haven't you?"

When she didn't answer immediately, he added quickly and more harshly, "Answer me, damn it. You've been sick, right?"

"Yes, yes," she said softly and her lips trembled. "I have but it's nothing. My stomach—"

"Has this happened before?"

"No, no," she shot back. But she had answered too hastily, and he knew she was lying.

"Well, once before . . ." She lowered her eyes.

"Once?"

She didn't answer—she didn't have to. He was making her very uncomfortable. She sighed heavily. "It's just that sometimes my stomach . . ."

"What stomach?" he challenged, crouched over the table. "You're probably to the point where you're having trouble keeping anything down . . ." He slowly reverted to his upright position; his eyes troubled and angry.

"Sure," he said, then slumped in his seat, "I should have guessed. I've seen you queasy before, but you always told me not to worry. It was either the heat or the excitement or good news—or bad news. Any excuse that would fit the moment." An exasperated sigh escaped his lips. "Tracy, Tracy, don't you realize I'm so worried about you; you're ruining your—"

"Mark, please don't," she interrupted him. "It's all this excitement and . . ."

Through tightly clenched teeth he uttered slowly and very deliberately, "Don't alibi yourself out of this one, Tracy. I'm the man who—who . . ." He was going to say Loves you, but couldn't bring himself to say it. He was so angry. Instead, he added, "Who worries about you." Again, he leaned across the table. "Admit it, it's happened more than a few times, hasn't it—hasn't it?"

"Yes!" She met his angry face with hers, the word coming from deep within her throat.

"Sure, I knew it. Now that I think about it—all those times we'd stop to eat. Once at that little roadside inn, where you said you had a headache and disappeared to take a pill; and the day we left

141

my place, and you said you were so happy and excited . . ."

Their eyes met, remembering the day, and the sharp memory of her body next to his was indelible in his mind. She was so tempting, so delicious, so demanding; and she was making herself sick.

He didn't want to experience the frustration—the knot in the pit of his stomach from wanting and caring. He wouldn't experience that kind of pain.

"Sure, even *that* day," he was continuing, knowing it was important and embedded in both their memories, "you gave me a lot of excuses when you didn't eat, and I was relegated to watching my dinner companion nibble on scallions and tomatoes . . ."

"Is that what I am to you—a dinner companion?" She jumped at the chance to be defensive because she knew, to a degree, he was right. "Well, have I been deluded!" she exclaimed in a harsh, annoyed voice. "I thought I meant a little more to you—"

"Stop it, Trace, you're twisting my words; you know what I mean!" His eyes suddenly reflected the hurt he felt at her caustic remark. "I'm worried," he said, calmer. "And I tried not to face it. But we weren't always together, and I couldn't tell if you were eating right. Oh, damn," he said disgustedly, "this isn't getting us anywhere . . ."

"You're right about one thing," she seethed. "This isn't getting us anywhere—and—if you can stop being so chauvinistic for a few minutes, I'd like to go home."

He looked back at her but said nothing. He stood and pulled her chair from beneath her. They both walked to the front of the restaurant, with fixed smiles on their faces, hiding their anger.

In the car his foot pushed heavily on the accelerator as he picked up the unfinished conversation. "Look at yourself. You're shaky right now, and your eyes are all watery. Don't you realize you can't go on like this?"

Tracy had just about had it with his badgering. "I haven't been going on 'like this'—whatever that means . . ."

"You know *exactly* what it means." He rolled the window down and let the cool air in. "Now that I think about all those times"—he took a deep breath—"that we had eaten—or rather, had *almost* eaten. And, you always had some lame excuse, and I, like the fool I was, always wanted to believe you. Now you've got to recognize it. You've pushed yourself to the point where your system rejects food—you're starving yourself. You know what's happening, don't you? Like those starving teen-agers who want to run around weightless."

"Well, I'm no teen-ager . . ."

"Then stop acting like one—damn it!" He glanced at her sharply. "You're heading for a classic case of anorexia nervosa and all so you'll be able to ride some damn horse!" He swerved and nearly went off the shoulder in the road. He was livid.

"You're just like everyone else—trying to tell me what to do," Tracy spat back at him. "I get it from all sides. Well, I have news for you, no one's perfect, not even you." She wanted to strike out at him, she was so upset. "Who do you think you are —a doctor?" She was flushed and shaking.

"No, I'm someone who . . ."

But she wasn't listening. She was stretching her

143

long, thin arms in front of her and pressing her hands against the dashboard as if to regain her strength. "Well, since we at least agree on *something*—that you're not a doctor—then I suggest you leave me alone!" She turned her face to him and her eyes were ablaze with hurt and anger.

"Gladly," he stormed, and pushed his foot down on the pedal. They didn't speak again for the short remainder of the ride. All Tracy could think of was that her world was falling apart. All those beautiful things he had said to her seemed to mean nothing now. Where had all those dreams and desires gone? Maybe she didn't know him as well as she thought. She had never seen him in such a temper. And she knew she was partly to blame.

He slammed the brakes on, and she nearly hit the dashboard. He looked straight ahead, his chiseled profile silhouetted in the darkness. He was so devastatingly handsome. This was not going according to her plans at all, and she knew it was her fault. The more she stared at him, the more she began to mellow. Finally, she relented, and knowing her voice was shaking, she spoke.

"Mark?" But he did not answer and stared into the night. Struggling to control her ragged breathing, she added, "I've been good for you, and you've been good for me . . ." But he made no attempt to communicate. "Well," she huffed, miffed at his lack of response, "good night *doctor!* And, I'll be damned if I'll apologize for anything." She opened the door and slammed it with all her might. He sat, like a stone idol, looking ahead, and she had had it. "And, sometimes, Mark Flanagan, you possess all the charm of an empty locker!" He took off without a backward glance.

CHAPTER SEVEN

Tracy threw herself into her riding and work-outs for the next few weeks, and she did not hear from Mark. Occasionally, she saw him at the track, but they avoided each other. Tracy was frantic. Her father and Scotty were more than a little concerned with the ferocity of her training.

On a cool Sunday morning Scotty walked through the back door of the house and peeked in the den. Tracy was sitting with her tea and the Sunday papers.

"You know what I think?" he said enthusiastically.

"Oh, hi Scotty," she said listlessly, looking up from the paper.

"I think"—he sashayed into the room with his hands in his pockets—"that a trip to California would do us all some good." And he said nothing more and hummed as he danced around the room, allowing the import of his suggestion to sink in.

Slowly, she dropped the paper to her lap and stared over her teacup. "California!" she screamed. "Santa Anita?"

"The one and only. Kenny has mounts for you, and I think that sunny California weather is just what you need to bring the roses back to those cheeks."

Tracy wasn't listening to his monologue, but kept repeating, "California, California." She jumped up and grabbed him, and they both danced around the room.

"I told the Bull this'd do the trick. Haven't been out there in a few years. But you'll love the track, lass. It's a beauty—and you're a winner. An unbeatable combination."

Maybe now, she thought, maybe now I can get him out of my system. But she really didn't want to —she longed for his touch.

The California reception was even greater than what she had received in Florida. They loved her and Tracy drove herself. She was down to ninety-eight pounds and even Scotty voiced his concern. True, she was riding great, he told her, but she could use a few extra pounds. She needed her strength to drive those ponies over the finish line. She casually dismissed his worries and told him as soon as they returned, she'd take it a little easier. But for now, let her enjoy her acclaim.

Her picture appeared in the Sports pages for days on end. She went to several parties and met some very interesting people, but she never stayed late. She was always up early the next morning, working out. Even Bull was enjoying himself, and they decided to extend their stay.

Tracy had mixed emotions; she loved the attention she was receiving, but she missed that face that haunted her. She was trying to eat, but big meals made her uncomfortable and queasy. She picked and devoured vitamins.

After a month of hectic pacing and riding the crest of her newfound popularity, Tracy and her entourage returned home.

As they rode from the airport in the rented limo, Tracy pretended to sleep. All the while she pictured Mark's deep-set eyes and tantalizing smile. Time did nothing to erase them but rather succeeded in engraving them ever deeper in the crevices of her mind. But why couldn't he understand? This was her career—what she had dreamed of all her life. She shifted in her seat and heard her father call out, "Well, here we are—home!"

As they drove up the driveway, a cold wind swept over the grounds and scattered the fallen leaves. The days were shorter now, and the early darkness brought with it a depression for Tracy. She couldn't wait for the next day, till she was back in the saddle; that seemed the only time she was able to forget and put him out of her mind.

"Here, Harry, she's all yours." Tracy handed the reins to the groom as a bracing wind whipped across the track. The sun had not yet risen, and the damp of night was still visible on the ground and trees.

"Coffee, Tracy?" Scotty offered his steaming brew from a Styrofoam cup.

"Just a sip, thanks. Boy, hope the sun comes up soon. It certainly is nippy." Tracy turned up the collar of her jacket.

"C'mon, Trace, let's go over to the stables. It's warmer there."

"Right." As she lifted her head, the first rays from the morning's sun broke across the wintry track. "Ah, it's going to be a sunny one, after all. Think I will have that cup of coffee," she said and shoved her hands deep into her pockets.

"Just think," said Scotty, heading up the incline,

"in another week, the Racing Commission will be honoring your father with that testimonial dinner. Forty years in the business. Now, that's some track record." He tossed his empty cup into the basket and adjusted his cap. "You should excuse the pun."

"I knew you couldn't resist that one, Buddha," she said with a smile.

He cleared his throat. "We've been hearing some good things about that Mark Flanagan fella." He shyly shot a look at Tracy, but received no reaction. She kept walking, her eyes straight ahead.

"Oh?" was all she said.

"Seems while we were away, he was busy. He's really getting into the business. Has a contingent of about nine fillies and ten colts—most of which will be ready in a couple of months." He rubbed the back of his neck and shook his head. "Sure beats the hell out of me—never would have expected it . . ."

"Goes to show you in this business there is no such thing as a sure thing." But there was a craving inside Tracy at the mention of his name; she realized that she felt empty. "Come on," she said, slipping her arm through his, "let's get some coffee."

The following Monday evening, some of the apprentice jockeys intended to go out and kick up their boots a bit since there was no action at the track the next day. Two of them asked Tracy to join them at a little Mexican restaurant nearby. They were probably feeling quite benevolent toward her, since Tracy had only ridden four mounts that day, and none of them had been in the money.

"Hey," Scotty had reprimanded her after looking at her dejected expression. "You can't win 'em all. Don't be so hard on yourself; we all have off days. Besides," he said and smiled elfishly, "the filly you ran in the sixth that you brought in fifth, well, she's been running consistently—last."

"Why, you devil," she yelled, tossing her boot at him. "You let me run some winded . . ."

"Not me." He put his hands up in front of him defensively. "Don't forget, Kenny's your agent—check with him. But, he must have had his reasons. You never can tell with these animals and"—he smiled—"ain't it grand that ya can't?"

"Oh, don't give me any of your stable philosophy . . ."

"Now, now, Trace," he said, rubbing her boot with his sleeve, "relax, will you? You've a day off tomorrow . . ."

So Tracy did just that: she relaxed and joined the two young apprentices who had asked her out. She felt more of an empathy with them than she did with the other veteran riders anyway. Besides, she was nervous; she knew Mark would be at the testimonial dinner for Bull in a few days. How she missed him.

Tuesday morning arrived and Tracy could barely get out of bed.

Tacos and wine—oh, my head! Oh, my weight! And she hit her forehead a little too energetically and paid the price. A small concert played in her head—and it was all brass!

After the cymbals ceased, Tracy eased herself from beneath the covers and tiptoed carefully to her scale. The bathroom light made her shudder. Through bleary red eyes, the tiny dial read one hundred. Relief calmed the abused stomach. She flipped off the light, headed for the bed, and

149

crawled back beneath the security of her covers, snuggling into a fetal position.

She was just beginning to drift off to sleep when a rap came to her door. "Go away," she mumbled thickly from her pillow, *"whatever* you are."

Heavy strides crossed her carpet and her slightly raised rear end was attacked by a not too gentle prodding of what felt like a wooden spoon, although in her present condition this morning, it seemed like a small battering ram.

"Hmmph," came sailing down to her on a breeze of onions and peppers.

She managed to open her eyes and peeked from beneath her security blanket. "Sally, please, can't you drive a truck through someone else's room?" She tried unsuccessfully to hide in the folds of her pillow. "Aren't they recruiting new S.S. officers somewhere else?"

"Very funny, your Royal Jockey-ness, but I've a household to run, and between the comings-and-goings of your father and the rest of them—and *you*—why, I never know when to . . ."

"All right, I surrender, I confess, I killed him, inspector . . ." This was greeted by another prod from her weapon, only much more heavily applied. "Okay, what is it?" she answered in a barely civil voice.

"Well, I have a roast beef today . . ."

Not food, she said to herself and clutched her stomach. Not so early.

". . . And it'll take at least two hours, so how long do you intend to sleep?" she continued.

"About a year and a half!" Muffled tones greeted the concerned cook. "Now leave me alone. I promise to be at muster whenever you say the

150

march should start and whenever I come to terms with my stomach."

"Hmm," the annoyed voice returned, heading for the door. "Just like your father . . ." and she slammed the door.

Tracy groaned and pulled a blanket over her head. She remained in her bed for the better part of that day.

"Tracy, come on," her father yelled from downstairs. "It doesn't look right for the guest of honor to be late."

"It does so," she shouted back. "You exude class when you arrive late; shows them how unconcerned and important you are."

Damn, she cried to herself, this zipper. Then she wiggled and it rode up smoothly. She was wearing a red-and-black full-length sheath with a daring slit cut high on her thigh. She dangled a long leg with a bright red sling, teasingly, from the slit, in front of the mirror.

"C'mon, Trace," her father bellowed.

"Okay, okay." She nearly forgot her purse as she ran down the stairs in anticipation of seeing Mark.

Tracy refused her father's request to sit at the podium with him. "It's your night," she told him. "I'll sit on the side with Gus and Scotty."

The place was crowded with guests. She craned her neck looking for him over the sea of faces. Tracy was receiving approving looks from many of the males present and a few jealous glances from the females. The dinner was served, and the presentation made, but still she hadn't seen him. Where is he? she asked herself. Suppose he didn't show? She wandered around speaking briefly to

151

some of the people she knew when a voice said, "Could I have this dance, miss?"

Tracy froze and stopped just as she was about to sip her drink. She turned slowly, exercising great control. "Why, Mark, I didn't know you were here," she said brightly, but her heart was beating furiously.

"Well, I was a little late," he said in a low voice, "so I stayed in the back; but I knew you were here. All eyes were on you." He took her hand. "Dance?" he asked again.

"Okay, why not?" she returned glibly.

They moved toward the crowded dance floor, and she slipped into his arms as if she had never been away. They danced together quietly in perfect unison.

After the first dance he relinquished his hold on her slightly and looked into her eyes. "Truce, Tracy?"

"Sounds like the title of a cheap espionage novel." She was so nervous, she was sure she would stutter.

He smiled. "Truce?" he repeated.

"Truce, Mark." She settled into his arms, enjoying his protective grip. She closed her eyes and she relaxed for the first time in weeks. He was gently rubbing his hand up and down her back.

"I see you've done well out on the coast, and since you've returned, I—Tracy—I . . ."

He was having difficulty and she was glad. He was as nervous and confused as she was. She looked up at him. "It's all right, Mark. I . . ."

"Tracy, I've missed you." He tightened the gap between them by squeezing her to him and whispered in her ear. "I must have picked up the

152

phone a hundred times. I can't say I'm sorry about . . ."

"Hush, Mark." She put her long, lacquered fingernail to his lips. "Let's not talk. Maybe we both have tempers that need quieting. Well, let's not talk about it yet. Just hold me close and dance—or I'll make a scene."

He simply smiled his answer and held her more tightly. Oh, Mark, she wanted to scream, take me away from this and make love to me. Be the man of my dreams again.

As if reading her mind, he whispered in her ear, "You know that little guest house of mine?"

"The one with all the loose shavings of wood, with sawdust on the floor—the one we never made it to that day?" She smiled and blushed all at the same time, remembering.

"Ah, the lady still blushes. How refreshing."

"It has something to do with my coloring . . ."

He laughed and whirled her quickly around the floor in a circle as the tempo of the music changed. "I was thinking devilish thoughts just now—like wouldn't it be nice to drive up there in the dark, and I could show you my . . ."

"Shavings?" she whispered back.

"Something like that." As the lights dimmed, his tongue found her ear and she thought she'd collapse. He was whisking her around the floor, the momentum gaining, and Tracy was dizzy with excitement. His muscular legs were pressing against hers.

"Yes, yes," she said. "I'd love to see your workshop; although I'm sure"—she continued and bit his ear playfully—"I'm supposed to be demure and more reserved and reticent in my reply. I suppose I should put you off and pretend . . ."

"I'm glad you're aggressive; I wouldn't have it any other way." His dark eyes held hers for what seemed to be an eternity.

"Let me get my bag and coat; I'll meet you in front," she said huskily.

The three bon vivants were still holding their wineglasses to the light and remained in heated discussion. Tracy slipped away unnoticed.

He drove with one arm on the wheel and one arm around her. They rode in silence. As his car slid into the driveway and turned in to the back of the house, he doused the lights and took her hand. There was a full moon that sent sporadic patches of light over the gravel. Tracy followed his lead, but had trouble navigating through the pebbles in her high heels. She took tiny, uncertain steps, one in front of the other, as if scouting a live mine field.

"Here," he said and turned. "This'll be easier." He picked her up swiftly and easily.

"Oh," she cried, "the air is so much thinner up here."

He leaned over and kissed her, squeezing her slim frame to him. Then he dropped her gently in front of the old white guest house. He unlocked the door and it made a tiny squeak.

"Enter," he said, "my home away from home."

It smelled of wood and glue. His smell was in here, too, Tracy realized. The shafts of moonlight made disparate patterns across his huge designing board and the cluttered floor. He reached for the light and Tracy stopped him.

"Don't, Mark, please, the moon is enough." She held his hand tightly as she surveyed the huge, comfortable room.

"And," he pointed, "right through there to the right is the kitchen. It's small but enough for my

154

purposes. And over here," he gestured to the left, "is the sitting room, the den—or whatever you want to call it." He ushered her in, and she was surprised at its size. There was a long sofa with pillows on it and an old mahogany coffee table in front of it. Across from it was a fireplace, which had been recently used. "Sometimes when I work late I sleep here," he said. "The couch pulls out."

There were a few more comfortable chairs, a bookcase, and lovely old oil lamps sitting on end tables on either side of the fireplace. Heavy mauve drapes covered the paneled walls. One set of drapes was partly opened and a shaft of moonlight darted across the floor, traveled up his body, and brushed across his tanned face. Tracy thought if he didn't take her in his arms soon, she'd go into some sort of fit. Surveying the room, she turned her back to him, and purposely leaned on him.

"It's—it's," she stumbled, looking for the word. "It's cozy—yes, that's it—cozy. No wonder you stay here . . ." His arm slid around her waist and pulled her closer to him. He leaned over and kissed her long white throat, and Tracy tilted her head back allowing her hair to fall away from her face, enjoying every hot caress. From her waist his hands worked up to her neck and then slid down to the deep crevice of her breasts. The low-cut gown was revealing, and he began to stroke the shiny fabric casually, just brushing it lightly with the tips of his fingers. It was a tantalizing maneuver and Tracy let a sigh escape.

"Mark . . ."

He turned her to him, slowly, and her eyes were bright and pleading. "Tracy . . ."

"There's just one thing," she said in a strained voice, looking up at him.

"Stipulations, yet?" He leaned over and pecked her on the lips, and continued nibbling down her neck to the top of her breast.

"Yes!" she blurted out.

Shocked, he held her at arm's length, waiting.

"Please—pull out the bed!"

He scooped her up and plopped her into one of the armchairs. "Don't move until I have everything ready." He pulled off his black jacket and threw it on her lap. With one flip he had the couch out. He reached in the closet and pulled out a pillow, sheet, and blanket. In seconds he had the bed made. He tossed the single pillow at the head of the bed. His face was flushed when he turned to her. "I'm afraid we'll have to share the pillow."

He beckoned to her. She stood and tossed his jacket aside, exposing a slim leg through the long slit of her dress. He was next to her in one swift stride. Rough fingers pushed the dress from her shoulders and he caressed the low part of her neck and then his tongue ran across her milky white shoulders. She moaned. And he continued lower, exploring the space between her firm breasts. Slowly, one hand crawled up her back to the zipper. He deftly pulled it down, and peeled the top of her dress till it fell to her waist. A low-cut black lace bra hugged her heaving bosom.

He gasped. "So long—so long, I've waited . . ." he was mumbling throatily. His right hand slipped around her waist and held her securely while his left crept, teasingly, inside the bra, searching for her nipple. He touched the nipple tenderly and then more forcefully when he felt it begin to harden. She sighed and opened her mouth to his. He whispered her name raggedly as their lips met. Seconds later he picked her up, carried her to the couch that had been converted to a bed, and lowered her into it. He lay on top of her and demanded that her squirming body stay still as he ran his hand down her exposed leg. Up and down the leg his fingers ran as his mouth pressed against hers, forcing it to stay open and feel the thrust of his tongue.

"Mark, Mark . . ." she managed to say when she had torn her mouth from his. Her fingers were tearing through his hair, holding his head down as he sought to run his tongue over her hot breasts. She lifted herself up to comply, and he unclasped the bra and slid it from beneath her taut body. Now he touched the tip of one pink nipple with his tongue and she writhed with pleasure. All she could do was call his name. He finished undressing her, slowly, wanting to savor every moment. He pulled her stockings off carefully and then leaned over her body, which appeared snow white in the moonlight, kissing it. He ripped off his shirt and her arms went out to him, stroking the bare sun-bronzed skin. She unbuckled his belt with tremulous fingers, and then he caught her hand and kissed it. With his other hand, he freed himself from his trousers.

She watched as he climbed nearer to her, his body almost shimmering in the pale light. He pinned her arms down with his hands as he lowered himself onto her. Her long hair was tossed across the pillow, carelessly, and her mouth was slightly open—moist and tempting—waiting to be assaulted.

At first he was tender, then he was more demanding, and finally passionately brutal. It was as if he was demanding recompense for all the lost hours. While he kissed her, he shifted slightly, allowing his hand to intimately explore the length of her body. He caressed the tender skin of her stomach and then gradually allowed his hand to slip between her thighs.

Her tiny moans turned into feverish gasps. He removed his hand and then pressed his body firmly on top of hers. She grabbed at him hungrily, starving for his love, and she wrapped her strong legs around him and pleaded, "Mark—Mark . . ."

"Not yet," he said roughly. "Not yet . . ."

His tongue was persistent as it plunged deeper and deeper into her receptive mouth. She returned the kiss as passionately as she could. They were both starved, longing for each other, their bodies craving erotic escape and the sexual release denied them because of their stubbornness. She dug into his bare, sweaty chest with her long, red nails, and he moved away slightly, straddling her. He looked down at her and murmured huskily, "Hellcat."

She looked up with heavy, slitted, sensual eyes, demanding more. "Mark . . ." Her tongue shot out and moistened her lips. It was an invitation, and he accepted it instantly and covered his mouth with hers, silencing her throaty request.

As she gasped, he rubbed his hot palm over her left breast, in rhythmic circles, at first slowly, and then faster, faster—gaining momentum. Her voice nearly exploded, she was so aroused, and her demanding tongue found his ear. His breath was hot on her neck and then his teeth bit into her soft, white flesh, erotically. His mouth was everywhere —devouring her, ravenous, his tongue thrusting like a red-hot saber; and they clung together frantically, demanding more of each other. "Now," he whispered brutally, "now you'll be mine."

They were one, and an explosion of stars and colors played inside Tracy's head, and she was being carried into a chasm of darkness. All thought vanished. There was nothing but him and this moment. She felt as if she had tripped on the precipice of eternity, and she was being tossed into a black velvety pit—never to return. And Tracy did not want to return, all she wanted was Mark. He was all the things she wanted, and she suddenly realized how his passion complied with her wishes, her needs, her demands—not just his own —and a feeling of happiness enveloped her.

They were nuzzled in each other's arms, and he had pulled the blanket up around them. He was tender and thoughtful, and Tracy loved that. "It gets a little chilly in here sometimes . . ."

"I doubt that," she said. "Not with you around me." She looked up impishly.

His index finger poked at her nose. "You are very, very sensual and seductive—and such a shy and retiring devil."

"I thought you liked your women aggressive . . ."

"Correction." He lowered his mouth to give her a series of quick smacks. "Woman—remember— woman. Why, I couldn't," he added, rolling away from her, "keep up with more than *one* like you . . ."

She tossed the pillow at him, and he caught it and tossed it back. She lifted herself on her elbow, holding the sheet against her breasts. "Well," she said sleepily, as he pulled on his shorts, "you could always make a fire. You said the fireplace works."

"Would you like that?" He half turned to her, looking over his shoulder, his hair a tousled mess.

"Umm, oh, yes." She snuggled herself into the pillow and hugged the covers around her.

"Then, a fire you shall have." He slipped his long-sleeved shirt on but left it unbuttoned, and Tracy took delight in watching him move around as he prepared the fire. His muscles rippled beneath his shirt as he sat on his haunches, fanning the fire. The fire was catching, and monstrous, shadowy figures danced inside the cozy room, landing on his back, the floor, and across their temporary bed. Tracy felt contented as the warmth from the fire colored her face.

He was poking at some old logs, and as the fire crackled, he called over his shoulder, "Can you cook, Sprite?"

"I don't know. I've never had to; and I'll be the first to admit, it's never been near the top of my priorities. Besides, I have Sally . . ."

He tossed his head back and laughed, nearly losing his balance. "A breed unto herself . . ." he mumbled.

She didn't quite hear him, and lifted herself from her supine position on a wobbly elbow. "You muttered something into that hairy chest?" she teased.

"Nothing important—" And then he brightened. "We might just want to eat alone sometime without outside help."

"Oh, is that a prerequisite for staying in your comfy, little hideaway?" She looked toward the kitchen.

He removed his shirt and stood over her, looking down into her face. Immediately, her pulse raced and her arms flew to him.

"Restraint, restraint," he said and smiled as he

160

climbed beneath the covers with her. He snuggled her next to him and they watched the roaring fire.

"Oh, this is delicious—almost sinful," she said and huddled closer. "I might even learn to cook . . ."

"It's all right; you really don't have to—I mean —it's just that I thought we could escape here."

"With that proposal open to me, I'll soon be a master chef."

He laughed and ruffled her hair as her slim, long fingers rubbed his chest under the covers and then her nails played across his tight stomach and then onto his thighs.

He leaned over and kissed her longingly, and she was so glad that neither of them had mentioned their last time together and their quarrel. Tracy did not like to waste energy on anger—she found it debilitating; she'd rather save her energy for this. She moaned fitfully as his hands groped for her—at first tenderly and then frantically. She returned his passion and massaged his body warmly as the fire roared and hissed, matching their heat, flooding the room with its glow until they—and it—succumbed to the quiet of smoldering embers.

Mark stared for a long time at the creamy white leg that was wrapped around the rumpled covers, and he had an uncontrollable urge to run his fingertips up and down the enticing limb. Just the top of her forehead and her thick, tangled hair could be seen peeking from above the blanket. He smiled at how she was wrapped like a tiny ball beneath the maze of twisted sheet and cover.

He slid from beneath his little corner of blanket carefully; he needed a cup of coffee.

Tracy's nose could not quite work free of the wrinkled sheet as it sought to discover the source of the disturbing aroma. She untangled one arm and thumped the covers behind her back only to discover empty space. Her eyes flew open. Looking at her new surroundings, she sighed and stretched. Then the scent drifted closer to her nostrils: coffee. "Ah," she yawned, and turned full on her back.

Mark heard her get up but he didn't move. He lifted the coffeepot and poured. "Do you want some coffee?" he asked, without turning around.

"Want it? I demand it!" she said.

His shoulders shook with laughter, and he turned with two mugs of steaming coffee in his hands.

Tracy was leaning against the doorjamb with her head tilted. The flowered sheet wrapped around her was tied beneath her left arm. Her left leg was partially exposed. The bright sunlight was playing around her hair and shoulders. Her arms were crossed at her waist, emphasizing the tight pull of the sheet across her breasts.

"I didn't mean to wake you, but I'm glad I did; that's quite a getup." He handed her the coffee.

She reached for the coffee, allowing more sheet to pull away, showing further thigh. "Well," she replied, "it beats a red-and-black sheath at . . ." She looked around the tiny sunlit kitchen. "No clock?"

"No clock," he replied to her milky thigh.

"Well, anyway, it beats sporting a red-and-black sheath at whatever time it is." She took a deep breath. "And stop looking at my leg like it was a side of beef. It makes me feel like you want your pound of flesh."

"Don't be so feisty; I'm bigger than you," he said and looked down at her upturned face and kissed her nose. "C'mon, let's sit inside." Then, looking around, he added, "Besides, we have no choice. There's no place to sit in the kitchen."

"All right," she said with a chuckle, "but take my cup while I attempt to tighten this Tracy Morgan original." He preceded her through the doorway, and she picked up the bottom of the sheet and threw it over her left shoulder, toga fashion.

He plopped on his side of the couch bed and put the coffee on the night table. He looked up and laughed heartily as she scooted to her side.

"Something amuses you?" she asked, crashing down beside him.

"Now you look like Mahatma Gandhi." He handed her the coffee.

"You're spoiling my image, you know. Besides, if you're going to keep seducing me in this manner, you could at least have a little something for me to jump into . . ."

"Seduce *you?* Why, you devil—if I ever saw lust in anyone's eyes . . ."

"That's not very gallant of you," she said, silencing him with her lips.

"You'd better not start, Trace," he said and released himself from her embrace and crossed the room, pulling back the drapes, allowing boundless sunlight to illuminate the room and dance over the swirling, disturbed dust.

"Oh, that's dirty pool." She put her arm across her eyes blocking the startling brightness. "A woman doesn't need to see the blinding sun first thing in the morning, especially when she's lying next to the man she . . ." Tracy bit her lower lip hesitatingly.

163

He snuggled in next to her and removed the arm gently from her eyes. "Say it, Tracy; say it in the harsh reality of the bright sunlight. Say it the way you can say it under the cover of darkness—say it," he demanded.

". . . loves." Her lower lip trembled and her arms went up and circled his neck, and she pulled his mouth down to hers.

He did not repeat her commitment, but he had said enough the night before to keep her happy for a long, long time. And she gave herself to him, again, willingly, and he teased her and tantalized her and drove her to heights of ecstasy.

His mouth covered hers as his hands ran over her breasts and tore the sheet away. He massaged her nipples till they were red and hard, and he looked down at the squirming, sensual body. He moaned, watching her, mesmerized. Then he slowly lowered himself onto her. Her hips were undulating, the rhythm driving him to even greater passion. He pressed himself on top of her, and they moved together silently—the only noise, the panting of their hot breath, and the sounds their writhing bodies made. Finally, she could stand no more and her arms closed around his neck and her long legs wrapped around him tightly. Like a hungry animal, she devoured him, and when she reached her apex, she shattered the silence and screamed his name. Tracy wanted nothing more than to experience his body for as long as she could. And she returned his passion with hers, her bruised mouth wanting more, her fingers digging and demanding. He took her to a state of rapturous delight till there was nothing but a black void dotted with shooting colors.

Tracy was beyond reason and self-control for his

lovemaking was overwhelming, and she was weak from emotion.

They played out their fantasies, content that they could both fulfill each other's demands, and then they plummeted back to reality and laid in each other's arms, silently, as the sun climbed higher over the little guest house.

CHAPTER EIGHT

For the next few months Tracy experienced a state of euphoria. She was riding the crest of popularity and totally enjoying it, and when Mark and she could, they escaped for a few days alone. It was now an open secret among Tracy's "family," but they respected her desire to keep her relationship to Mark as private as possible. All they knew was that she had never looked happier—or ridden better—and no one was going to disturb that combination. She was bringing the horses in, and big money was at stake.

She was eating a little better, especially around Mark, but she went on periodic fasts whenever she gained a few pounds or he wasn't around. He hadn't mentioned her eating habits for a long time, for which she was grateful. She had arranged her own schedule: if she ate lunch with him on her free day, there was no dinner or vice versa. He knew she could never eat before a race, so he didn't bother her on that account. In fact, he was becoming so wrapped up in his own stable that she didn't see as much of him as she had wanted. But, she had her own career, and it was booming. All she could see in the distance was the Kentucky Derby; and that was coming in only six weeks. She definitely had to watch her weight now.

Much to Sally's amazement, Tracy was hanging around in the kitchen more than she had in her entire life. Tracy had attempted, unsuccessfully, to make Mark an omelet in their hideaway, and it had been a dismal failure. She asked Sally questions and watched as she worked in the kitchen.

Tracy sat on a breakfast stool, her knees raised to meet her chin, her eyes darting, following the huge figure as she bent, straddled, heaved, stretched, and hummed—never breaking stride.

Sally was basking in the attention Tracy was paying her, and her gruffness mellowed as Tracy watched, entranced, while the huge form whipped up a sizable cake batter.

A tiny voice escaped Tracy's lips, her arms clasped tightly around her legs, her chin still supported by her knees. "Sally?" The wide eyes opened.

"Yes?"

"Promise"—she sighed—"promise you'll never leave us!" And the huge eyes surveyed her imploringly.

And the hulking, perspiring form just tossed her head back and bellowed, realizing she was receiving the greatest of compliments from the slim enigma sitting astride her stool.

"I promise, luv, I promise." She laughed, wiping the tears of amusement from her eyes with the back of her flour-coated hand. "You always could make me laugh." Then she cleared her throat. "Can I fix you something, Trace?"

"No, no, I'm riding this afternoon. I'll just have some juice," she said and slipped from her perch.

"Well." The hefty figure straightened, a little more serious now. "Who can keep up with the

167

schedule of this household?" And she began beating the dough unmercifully.

"Right," Tracy replied and left her to her frantic gyrations.

Saturday at the track was always an exciting day. It was more crowded than usual. Some of the best mounts, because of the crowd, ran on Saturdays. Tracy was all dressed in her green-and-white silks and weighed in, with her hair tucked securely beneath her cap, following Scotty to the paddock.

"Now remember this filly, lass, she likes to pull to the right—so watch her . . ." But Tracy was paying no attention. She was waving to the tall figure who was hurriedly walking toward her. "Oh, sure, Scott, sure—pulls to the right—I'll remember," but she was walking in the other direction to meet Mark.

He towered over her and gave her that smile that set her silks on fire. They didn't touch—there were too many people around—but their eyes said it all.

"If I didn't know better, I'd swear you were somebody's kid brother."

"If you care to step behind the barns, I'll prove you wrong. Better still, I'll wait till later, when we're—"

He cut her off. "I'm sorry, Sprite, that's what I came to tell you. I won't be able to see you tonight."

Tracy was sorely disappointed. She had planned to surprise him with her newfound culinary arts. She was going to cook a roast beef—a real home-cooked dinner—or so she hoped. She had everything down pat from Sally, and she was looking forward to showing him her domestic side, if she possessed one.

"Do I have competition?" she asked, trying to keep her voice light.

"Yes, to borrow your phrase, and it has four legs . . ."

"Oh."

"Yes, I have to take a run over to Brady's farm to look at a colt that Fred saw. He sounds like a winner." He paused, realizing she wasn't joining in his enthusiasm. "Trace? What's the matter? We'll have all day tomorrow . . ."

"Right," she said and raised her head. "Tomorrow—then," and she turned to go.

"Tracy," he called and she stopped. He walked next to her and steered her away from the noisy crowd toward a shed, where they at least enjoyed some privacy. "What's the matter?" he asked, placing his hands on her shoulders. "You knew this was coming up."

"I just didn't expect it today."

"Well, neither did I—but . . ."

She turned at him, furious with herself for being agitated, and furious with him for spoiling her surprise. She nervously tucked her shirt inside her pants and looked up at him. "Anyway, what is this newfound love you've developed for horses? A few months ago you didn't seem to know the nose from the tail. What prompted this?"

"You!" His cool voice returned without hesitation.

"Thanks, I needed that," she said and removed her hand that had been shielding her eyes from the sun. She felt about three feet tall.

"I'm sorry, Mark, it's just that I had a surprise planned, and—"

"And, I repeat, can we do it tomorrow? You're not riding, are you?"

169

"No, but"—she paused, a twinkle in her eyes—"I could be talked into it."

"You are a terrible tease, but if it's any consolation, I'd *much* rather be with you than traipsing through Brady's barns." Then he smiled. "Heaven help me, I think I'm getting used to you."

She smiled in return. "Be careful with those proclamations, they could be dangerous." All the tension lines left her face.

"Yes, I know. But I just can't seem to help myself when I'm around you; besides, I only make these announcements with careless abandon when no one else is within earshot."

"Coward," she replied.

"Right." He reached down and pulled her cap off, allowing her hair to tumble freely. "Now I know you're not the boy next door."

"Why you—" She was cut off by the bellows from her trainer. "C'mon, Tracy. They're almost ready for you."

"Okay, okay," she yelled in return, stuffing her hair back beneath her cap. Then, turning to Mark, she winked. "My public." And in a lower voice said, "Okay, we'll do it tomorrow. Five o'clock at the hideaway—not a minute before. I want everything to be just right."

"Okay, I won't be a minute sooner. Go now, to your public."

"Eat your heart out." She blew him a kiss and scooted toward the noise and the action. Mark watched the slim figure as the familiar voice called, "Riders up!"

The excited voices were yelling, "C'mon, Tracy, bring in a winner," and "that's Bull Morgan's kid, all right . . . ." Tracy rode out onto the track, experiencing the elation that always filled her when a

170

challenge faced her. I'll show him, she thought, I'll show 'em all.

At ten after five he walked through the door, and Tracy was so nervous you would have thought she was about to give birth. She heard the creaky door and knew he had stepped inside. "Don't you dare come into my kitchen," she screamed. The little room looked like a tornado had whipped through it and had only spared a wobbly roast beef atop a blood-soaked breadboard, a small casserole of tiny peas and pearl onions topped with almonds, and a stately spinach salad.

"Damn, damn, damn," she exclaimed, trying to control and slice the roast beef that definitely seemed to have a mind of its own as it attempted to slide from its moist launching pad.

"Can I help?" he yelled from inside as he flipped on the radio.

"Don't you dare come through that door," she screamed.

He laughed and said no more.

Ten minutes later they both sat cross-legged on pillows in front of the coffee table that she had transformed into a dining area through Sally's tablecloth and costly Waterford crystal. They toasted and Mark sliced through his beef.

She watched in anticipation, clutching her knife and fork defensively.

"Umm, not bad, not bad." He chewed, smiled, and swallowed.

Tracy figured he was just trying to be nice, but when she released her death grip on her "weapons" and cut through her piece, she tasted and brightened. "Not bad, is it?" And she ate another mouthful, surprised at her good luck.

171

"In fact," he said, attacking the vegetables, "everything is very good."

Tracy beamed, and as she watched him, she added, "Guess what?"

"You mean, there's more?"

"Of course. There's dessert."

Now he sat back and looked up in surprise and pointed to her. "You? Dessert?" His eyes rolled toward the ceiling. "I know. It's going to be cottage cheese over melba toast."

"No, Smarty, it's ice cream. . . ."

He placed his elbows on the table and stared at her. "Ice cream?" He gulped some ice water. "I never thought I'd see the day that Tracy Morgan would—you mean"—he paused for effect—"you really *like* ice cream?"

"Okay, okay, back off—I've got your message." Then she leaned across the table and said in a low tone, "I'll have you know, I'd *kill* for ice cream!" and she bared her teeth.

He exploded with laughter and stretched his legs beneath the table. Tracy cleared the dishes and served her favorite, strawberry ice cream.

After she put all the dishes in the sink, vowing to do them later, they snuggled together on the couch. He sipped coffee; she sipped her herbal tea.

"Tracy, I have to hand it to you, that was delicious."

"You're devastated by my culinary talents, are you?"

"Well, I wouldn't say 'devasted'—surprised is more like it."

"I'll let you in on a little secret—I'm not only surprised, I'm amazed."

"And you actually ate an entire meal," he said and smiled down at her, nuzzled comfortably in the crook of his arm. "I haven't wanted to mention it—because, well, things were going so well—but I'm always concerned about your eating habits. I'm not with you all the time and I don't know what you do . . ."

Her stomach was becoming upset. She wasn't enjoying the turn his conversation was taking. "Look, Mark, we've been through this before. You don't have to watch over me and check what I eat. You're not my father," she paused, "*or* my husband. You know it's important that I keep my weight down or I won't be able to ride, so let's let it be."

"But you can't go on forever, picking and starving yourself." He turned to her and put his coffee down.

"I am *not* starving myself, damn it," and then she felt it. The sick feeling continued to well up inside her. She fought to keep it down. "How can you say that after seeing me put away that meal like a truck driver."

"I'll admit"—he was sitting with one foot crossed over his knee, pulling at the top of his sock —"you ate better than usual, but still . . ."

"Let's change the subject."

"Okay," he said with a sigh, "topic changed." But he had a faraway look that she didn't like. He had been terribly moody the past few weeks, and when she had asked him if there was something wrong, he would just snap a sharp no in reply. Tracy didn't want to pry; everyone needed some privacy. She was so crazy in love with him that she made any allowance that would keep peace and keep him with her.

Suddenly, he brightened. "I might be able to

enter King's Row in the derby. Looks like she's ready."

"Why, you sly ol' fox." She looked at him and pushed him at arm's length. "You never mentioned anything to me. That's wonderful."

"Well, you've been so busy, riding and *winning*," he said and winked, "but actually, I wasn't too sure until the other day. She looks good."

"You mean"—she toyed with the button on his shirt—"you're going to be competing against me and Becket?"

"Well, we'll certainly give you a run for your money."

"No problem." She moistened her lips. "I love a challenge!"

"I know," he said huskily, and he stretched his arm and turned out the light, pitching them in darkness except for the tiny glimmer thrown by the kitchen light. Tracy thought of all those pots and pans and sighed, wishing Sally could materialize.

"But, the dishes . . ." she uttered through muffled tones.

"I've decided I don't *love* you for your domesticity, Trace; your talents lie in other directions." He pushed her down on the long couch and laid next to her. "And, there'll be no bed pulled out right now; you can't have your way all the time."

As the darkness enveloped them, he slowly undid the buttons of her blouse, feeling her breasts beneath the thin material. Then he slid inside her bra and played with her, slowly, sensually. He needed her, but he wanted it to be slow—slow and deliberate—experiencing every little detail of her.

She started to grope for him and he stopped her. "Do nothing," he whispered, "I'm going to drive

174

you wild slowly. You're mine and I want to enjoy you."

He slid his fingers from her breasts, lowered his mouth, and let his tongue flick across her breasts. Then his mouth closed over her nipple and his right hand traveled down to her jeans and he pulled down the zipper and slipped his hand inside. She began to tremble; his mouth still on her breast, demanding. She arched her back and he pulled down her pants and thrust his hand between her legs. She screamed and his mouth roughly closed over hers, quieting her. Finally, he peeled off her blouse and finished undressing her, and again her arms reached up for him, pleading, grabbing at his belt, and this time he let her. They were both stripped of clothes and inhibitions. He straddled her, burning to be inside of her as he lowered himself to her twisting body.

This time he was rough with her and demanding, and she returned his heat with her own demands and needs as she hung onto that lovely four-letter word, love. They were two passionate souls, giving themselves up to the heat of the moment—and each returned and satisfied, unquestioningly, the other's wants.

Much later he pulled out the bed, and they collapsed into it, and in a minute Mark was in a deep sleep. But Tracy's stomach would not be still, and she slipped quietly from the bed and went out the tiny back door and was sick. She climbed stealthfully back into the bed as he sleepily called her name.

"I'm here, Mark, I'm here." She, too, fell into a fitful sleep.

CHAPTER NINE

For the next few weeks Tracy put herself through rigorous training, and when Mark was traveling, she was even more strenuous in her endeavors. She trained and exercised all the harder because she missed him so. Her nerves were so bad that she could eat very little. But at least he wasn't around to witness her "nervous" appetite. She knew, however, that she wasn't feeling up to par.

A week before the derby Scotty threw a little garden party to celebrate the upcoming event. It was a rather noisy and boisterous affair with loud music and dancing, and there were trainers, owners, and jockeys everywhere. It was a great way for everyone to let off some steam.

Mark arrived late and Tracy didn't see him. He had been away for a week and she was frantic. When he sidled up behind her and kissed her on the ear, she whirled around.

"Expecting someone else perhaps?"

"No, no," she said, overjoyed to see him. Her hand drifted automatically to his side and he clasped it.

"It's great to see you; I was afraid you wouldn't make it."

"What? And miss Sally's homemade potato salad? Never!"

"That's not exactly what I wanted to hear, mister; men have been killed for less."

"Come," he said and laughed, "let's move away from all these gyrating bodies; there's only *one* I'm interested in . . ."

"Lecher," she said and followed him toward a stand of weeping willows and tall hedges.

"Besides," he added, ducking to avoid the drooping branches of the trees, "I tried to call you yesterday, but Sally said you were busy . . ." He steered her by the wrist toward the protection of the trees. It was lovely and cool—and private.

"I—I was running Becket through her paces." She leaned against the tree, looking up at him. She moistened her lips as he looked at her. "I think I've got a winner—I'm so excited, Mark; she is a true thoroughbred and reacting beautifully . . ."

He had his hands on her shoulders, looking down at her. "Trace, you're not overdoing it, are you? After all, you need some rest, too."

"I'll have plenty of time to rest *after* I win the derby," she said with an air of assurance.

"Such confidence." He toyed with her hair.

"And—don't you think I can win? You're not just a little jealous just because you have an entry now yourself, are you?"

His eyes narrowed. "Don't be ridiculous . . ." He saw her wink, and he knew she had been goading him. He leaned over and kissed her passionately, and her arms slipped automatically, instinctively, around his neck as he locked her in a long, brutal kiss. His hand slowly inched up to cup her breast and tiny gasps escaped her. Then he pulled back and looked at her. "Oh, that mouth," he murmured.

Her parted lips opened to his conquest. "Mark,"

she cried. He inched closer to her, his legs pressing hers to the huge tree and finally she moaned, "Mark, someone might . . ."

"Quiet," he said huskily and her mouth opened eagerly to accept his hot, plundering tongue as it dueled and played with hers. Slowly, he withdrew.

"Oh, how I missed that," she panted.

The noise from the crowd intruded and he pulled away and stared down at her. "Okay, I'll behave." He paused. "But, another thing you do to me is make me ravenous—for food. How about joining me for some of that fare over there?" And he pointed to the huge display of food on long tables.

"Well," she said with a sigh, "I already sampled a little of everything . . ."

"I bet it was a *little*," he said. .

"What's that supposed to mean?" Her eyes widened and she pushed herself from the tree with her boot.

"Just that you look thinner than ever."

"Don't start, Mark," she pleaded.

"Tracy, I'm tired of fencing with you. God knows, I missed you terribly this past week, and when I do come back, I see how thin and pale you look. I know you've been training very hard, but you look so awfully tired—"

"So, maybe you shouldn't leave me so often, especially when the derby's coming due."

"Let's not get on that kick again." He tried to keep the edge out of his voice. "You know it's business, and if I could have avoided it—"

"Yes, yes, we know what an entrepreneur you've become." She turned her back on him. He whirled her around to him.

"Tracy, stop it. You do look pale, damn it—in

178

fact, you don't look good at all! Maybe the people around you can't see it, but I can, because I've been away. After all, the derby is demanding; are you sure you're up to this? There's always another—"

She pulled away from him. "What are you trying to say?" She took several steps backward. "Spit it out . . ."

"Well, there's always next year, and it's—"

"Next year? Next year?" Her eyes widened in disbelief.

"Calm down, Tracy, I was only thinking out loud."

"Well, think out loud in the privacy of your own room." She felt tears in her eyes and she fought to keep them back. "Well, I won't calm down!"

"Tracy, I'm sorry, I only meant—"

"It's *very* clear just what you meant." She threw her head back defiantly and tucked in her shirt. "Sometimes, Mr. Flanagan, I think you have a perverted sense of humor. After I've worked and slaved, you have the temerity to even *breathe* those words—how dare you!"

"Stop acting like a prima donna," he exclaimed. "I can't seem to say anything to you anymore without you going crazy. The minute I show my concern, you twist everything . . . damn it, Tracy, grow up and recognize when someone is concerned and trying to help."

"Well, just forget about your concern. And if you'll excuse me, I'm going to join some friends who really are *concerned,* because they happen to think I can win the derby!"

She turned, her head held high and imperiously,

and hastened toward the boisterous crowd. She joined the throng of party-goers as the silent figure was left to stand beneath the lonely weeping willows.

CHAPTER TEN

The hot sun was smiling down on the day of the derby, sanctioning the event. Beautiful women, monied owners, and die-hard fans filled the park. There was a circus atmosphere everywhere and Tracy stood outside the paddock, her palms sweating, looking for the face she hadn't seen in a week. Because of their last encounter, she was in a worse state than she'd thought possible. Never did she think she could miss someone so much.

"Hey, lass," Scotty was calling to her, "look at those odds," pointing to the TV screen in the paddock area. "Misty Island is the favorite with our Becket running a close second."

Tracy looked up at the screen and saw that Mark's horse, King's Row, was a thirty-to-one shot. Mark Flanagan was still a bit of an outsider as far as most of the other more established owners were concerned. He had yet to prove himself.

Tracy was beside herself. She couldn't see him anywhere, which she thought was just as well because she was down to ninety-six pounds. Even her father and Scotty were both worried. She was having a devil of a time holding anything on her stomach; and she knew it was more than the expectation of the impending race. She was also experiencing occasional dizzy spells.

"Take it easy"—Scotty interrupted her private thoughts—"with Becket today; she's primed and ready, lass."

Then the formidable form of her father was looming over her. "Well, Tracy, baby, this is it. You've done it—what you've always wanted." He took her by the shoulders. "Your mother would have been proud," he said and paused, "and you know *I* am. Now, be careful . . ." His thick calloused fingers wiped a tear in the corner of his eye and he ran a wrinkled hanky over his flushed face as Scotty led her to the Riders Circle.

"Riders Up!" A burst of applause and cries filled the area. Tracy rode as if in a trance, unable to believe that her dream was materializing. The jockeys rode their horses proudly around the Riders Circle as anxious spectators good-naturedly yelled their demands at their favorites. There was much cajoling and heckling, and the crowd's enthusiasm was electric. The excitement was contagious and Tracy's stomach was doing flips.

A far-off voice was announcing: *"And the horses are on the track."* As they were guided by their outriders onto the track, the traditional strains of "My Old Kentucky Home" was playing in the background. Some of the horses bucked and wanted to race ahead, but the outriders kept them in check. Anxiety and expectation filled the air, and even the animals seemed to sense it.

They paraded back and forth in front of the stands and all eyes were on them. As they approached the gate, the assistant starters led the horses into their respective posts.

The voice was again booming into the mike: *"It is now post time . . ."*

The field was now in the hands of the starter,

and he bellowed orders at the jockeys, shouting for them to control their mounts. Nervous, some of the horses pawed the dirt, while others strained at the bits, stretching their necks, whinnying.

There was an urgency to the moment. Tracy's mouth went dry and shivers traveled up and down her spine. This was it—this was Churchill Downs and the Kentucky Derby. She steadied the nervous Becket with her left hand and waited for that final call.

A hush fell over the crowd as the speaker cracked: *"And, they're off!"* Then pandemonium broke loose—screams were heard from every corner of the clubhouse, right down through the grand stand.

Tracy broke with the pack and saw she was fifth in the field, in the middle of the track, just about where she wanted to be. The race was a mile and a quarter, and as Becket rounded the first turn, Tracy felt almost lightheaded. She shook her head, trying to dispel the feeling. *You'll wind up very sick . . .* a pleading voice was intermingling with the noise of the stampeding horses. She dug deeper into the stirrups and hung onto Becket, imploring, "You can do it, baby, show 'em." But she had a tough time concentrating; the combination of the pressure to win the race, together with her recent upset with Mark, produced an emotional state that had her at a fever pitch. Her vision was now blurred.

At the half Becket was running easily, and she closed ground and moved into third place. But she felt nauseous, and the double vision returned. Tracy clung tighter to the reins and took several deep breaths, trying to clear her head.

At the far turn Tracy's head cleared and she dug

in and rode, oblivious to all the noise and hoopla around her. But as they approached the stretch, her vision blurred again and she held on to Becket for dear life. For a fleeting moment she thought she'd lose control of her horse. For the first time since she had started riding, she was frightened. In the stretch they were crowding her and Tracy felt weak, but she managed to guide Becket. She finally brought the whip down and implored the horse to go faster. Her eyes misted and sweat covered her face. She heard screams and saw vague figures jumping in the stands as she raced by. She heard herself yell, "Do it, Becket." Then she heard another distant voice calling: *"And that's it, ladies and gentlemen."* The announcer was screaming, *"King's Row, a long shot, winner by a nose; Becket a close second."*

That's all Tracy heard of the call. She was devastated—second! She hugged the horse tightly, for if she didn't, she would have fallen off. And Tracy realized she was drained and debilitated—another dream shot. First, Mark—now her derby.

Everyone was surrounding her; they thought she had done great. A woman jockey coming in second in the Kentucky Derby! They were hugging and squeezing her. But the noise and heat was too much. She slipped away, telling her father she needed a little breathing space for a few minutes. But, as she walked away, the last thing she remembered was Harry's happy face smiling at her as she nearly walked into him, and the ground came up to meet her.

Tracy had been in the hospital for three days suffering from exhaustion. She also had much time to think. The first day they had fed her intravenously; the second day, liquids and light food; and today, a thick broth ladened with noodles.

The doctor was an old Southerner with white hair, half-glasses, and soft gray eyes. "When was the last time you ate a decent meal, young lady?" He peered at her from his "Ben Franklin's." He raised his hand as she began to speak. "And, no lies or excuses—I've heard them all before. And—I've seen these symptoms before."

"Well . . ." Tracy lowered her eyes and played with the corner of the sheet.

"Just as I thought," he said with a sigh. "You haven't eaten anything solid in weeks, have you? And," he added, "it's become more difficult to keep food down?"

"Yes," she said in a tiny voice, avoiding his eyes.

He patted her knee through the sheet, and said, "Luckily we caught you in time." He paused. "I've told the Press," he began and Tracy looked at him in horror. Seeing her anxiety, he said, "Not to worry, Miss Morgan, I've told them you're suffering from exhaustion and that you'll be up in the saddle soon." She sighed her appreciation and he smiled. "You're a very, very popular young lady— and pretty, too."

Tracy blushed. "Thank you, doctor."

He cleared his throat and straightened his back. "You do know what you've nearly slipped into, don't you?" Before she could answer, he added, "Anorexia nervosa—which can be fatal." Then, more sternly he said, "You can't ride if you're sick." Tears appeared in her eyes, and he dabbed at them with a tissue. "We don't want you to dehydrate, too. This will remain our secret, Miss Morgan—"

"Tracy, please," she interrupted him.

185

"Besides, Tracy," he said with a smile, "you come from a good stock, so I'm not going to worry about you." As he got up to leave, he asked, "I really *won't* have to worry, will I?" She shook her head in agreement.

"But," he continued, "it must be *your* decision. Think about it. I could lecture you for hours, but that would do no good. I'm sure you'll make the right decision. Don't forget, few people have experienced what you have in such a short time, young lady. Why"—he smiled again—"you're a celebrity, and *still* on top!" She caught his drift and smiled her appreciation.

"Oh, by the way, you have a visitor; he's been waiting all day to see you." He turned and walked from the room.

As Mark walked through the door, the first thing Tracy noticed was the tired, strained face. She was so happy to see him; but after their last meeting, she wasn't sure of how to approach him. She swallowed. "Congratulations," she said, "you're now one of the horsey set." She tried to sound cheerful. He looked so forlorn.

He let out an exasperated sigh and looked at her warily. "Yes, I suppose that does make it official . . ." He paused and continued to stare at her. Tracy felt very uncomfortable; the tension was almost palpable. Finally, he cleared his throat, and added off-handedly, "And, you should be very proud; the first woman jockey to come in at the Kentucky Derby. Everyone's still talking about it." But there was no joy in his voice. She saw how tired and dejected he looked and knew it was all her fault! Suddenly, nothing seemed to matter but him. She attempted to break the tension. She wanted to appease him and make all the animosity disappear.

"Well, doesn't the lady jockey deserve a little kiss for being in the money?" she asked, playing with the sheet.

He sighed. "Tracy, I'm a little too tired to be playing games. These last few days have been hell for me; I'm so exhausted . . ."

"I know, I can see it, but things are going to be better." She brightened, and added, "Why I've just received a clean bill of health from the doctor —he says I'm suffering from exhaustion and—"

He cut her off abruptly. "We both know what you're suffering from, Tracy. The doctor, your father, and I had a long talk."

She reddened. "But he said he wouldn't tell anyone."

"I thought I rated a little higher than anyone, Tracy."

She turned her head to the window and bit her lip. "Oh, Mark, I'm so sorry. I never meant . . ." Silent tears assailed her cheeks.

"Look, Tracy"—he slumped down on the bed next to her, studying his hands while she faced the window—"I haven't slept in two nights worrying about you. I've had time to think. I couldn't stop you from doing what you wanted. Maybe I *was* too overbearing, but I only wanted what was best for you. Maybe I was jealous of your preoccupation with your horses. . . . I don't know; I don't have all the answers." He turned and looked at her. "You do what you want; I'm tired. But I just can't stand by and watch you destroy yourself."

"But, I'm not—"

He didn't let her finish. "It's funny, I threw myself into this game because I was so crazy about

187

you; now I'm one of your"—he smiled more amiably—"horsey set. But, damn it, I needed you and you were always so involved with your horses." He was beginning to raise his voice. "When you kept asking me what was bugging me the last few weeks, I didn't want to bother you because I knew you were under such pressure. The designs I sent to the manufacturer for my boat had been turned down. They needed more detail; well, damn it, I had no time to give them *more* detail. I was wrapped up in my stables and—and *you!* Well," he continued, his face red, "I'll admit it, I needed some moral support, but you were always so involved, and"—he paused, letting a sigh escape—"I guess I'm just letting off a lot of steam, but Trace, you'd make such a damned good trainer." The beginnings of a smile curled his lips.

Slowly, the tension dissolved between them as he reached for her hand. Now Tracy realized how self-centered she had been. She was so engrossed with her own career and feelings that she had given little time to what he might have been experiencing and what *he* might have wanted. She just assumed everything was going to be all right for him. How could she have been so obtuse? She had acted like a spoiled, selfish brat! But now, silently, looking into his eyes for those fleeting moments, she had made her decision. She raised herself on her elbows and looked at him.

"Mark, will you do me one little favor?"

"I don't know if I have the strength; you're too demanding," he said solemnly. She could see his furrowed brow and the worried look in his eyes. "But"—he sighed—"I'll try."

"You can handle this one." She squeezed his hand. "Would you please go out and get me a cheeseburger with onions, french fries, and a malted milk? We trainers need to keep up our strength, you know." She settled back into her pillows.

He looked into her eyes and knew she wasn't kidding, and suddenly all the tension between them melted. "Tracy—Tracy—honest?" His face shone and all the tired worry lines vanished. "I can't believe it—you mean it?" She nodded enthusiastically. And they both spoke at once, animatedly, laughing in their excitement.

"Why, you wonderful, unpredictable devil, you. You've taken light-years off my life . . ."

"Believe me"—she touched his face—"I need you more than I need any horse."

For a long moment they just sat, holding hands. Finally, he gave her his infamous smile. "And you know something? You'll cost so much less to feed—Mrs. Flanagan."

"Mrs. Flanagan? Mrs. Flanagan?" She gasped, eyes opened wide. "I can't believe it . . ."

"Believe it," he said with a smile. "Besides, I've had it," he said, rubbing his back. "I can't take that convertible bed much longer. I'm opening up the master bedroom, and letting all the ghosts out, and taking a trainer in."

"Oh, Mark, Mark, I'm so happy. I've so much to make up to you. I should have been more concerned with your—"

"Tracy, Tracy," he said, putting his finger to her lips, "we both have a lot to learn, but we've got a lifetime to do it." He paused. "I never meant to interfere—or dominate you, Trace."

"Oh, Mark," she screamed, "I'm so happy! Dominate me—dominate me! And, don't forget," she added, breathlessly, "I've also had time to think

189

and reflect while I've been in here. I've been more fortunate than most; I've had my day in the sun. I've come in second in the derby. How many jockies do that? And now . . . now, I'm ready to face reality. But remember, it's better to retire a winner than to hang around and become a loser!"

"Such profound philosophy," he teased.

"Right—so now I'm ready to train, train, train—and with a ring on my finger. Oh, I'm so happy, Mark; but"—she pushed him back slightly and winked—"I only came in second . . ."

He looked at the radiant face and he leaned over and kissed her eyes and then her mouth tenderly. As they touched lovingly, he whispered softly, "With me, Trace, you'll always be a winner —and you'll always come in first!"

190